MW01580864

THE FANTASTIC FREEWHEELER

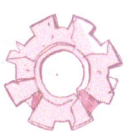

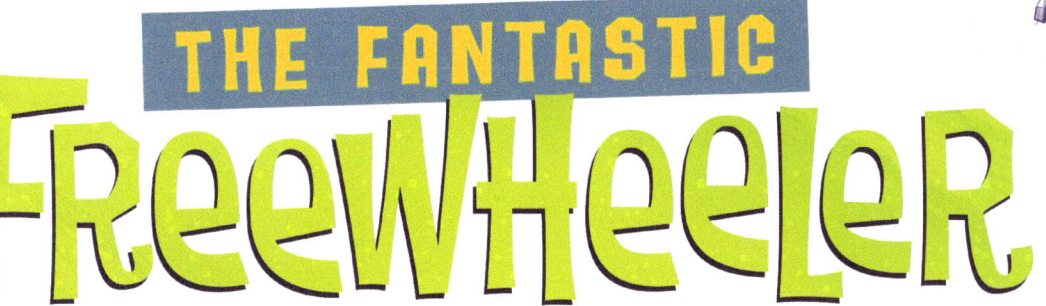

Published by Stone Arch Books, an imprint of Capstone
1710 Roe Crest Drive, North Mankato, Minnesota 56003
capstonepub.com

Copyright © 2024 by Capstone. All rights reserved. No part of this publication may be reproduced in whole or in part, or stored in a retrieval system, or transmitted in any form or by any means, electronic, mechanical, photocopying, recording, or otherwise, without written permission of the publisher.

Library of Congress Cataloging-in-Publication Data
Names: Felder, Molly, author. | Guzman, Yury, illustrator. | Brown, Scott (Illustrator), illustrator.
Title: The Fantastic Freewheeler and the mega bot attack : a graphic novel / written by Molly Felder ; art by Rory Walker ; cover art by Scott Brown.
Description: North Mankato, Minnesota : Stone Arch Books, [2023] | Series: The Fantastic Freewheeler | Audience: Ages 8-12 | Audience: Grades 4-6 | Summary: Drew Daniels, aka the Fantastic Freewheeler, is paired up with unlikable Brent Baker, who hijacks their science project to build a mega robot that goes haywire, so Freewheeler uses his superpowers to figure out how to stop the destructive construction.
Identifiers: LCCN 2023001423 (print) | LCCN 2023001424 (ebook) | ISBN 9781669012283 (hardcover) | ISBN 9781669012238 (paperback) | ISBN 9781669012245 (pdf) | ISBN 9781669012269 (kindle edition) | ISBN 9781669012276 (epub)
Subjects: CYAC: Graphic novels. | Superheroes—Fiction. | People with disabilities—Fiction. | Science projects—Fiction. | Cerebral palsy—Fiction. | LCGFT: Superhero comics. | Graphic novels.
Classification: LCC PZ7.7.F454 Fac 2023 (print) | LCC PZ7.7.F454 (ebook) | DDC 741.5/973—dc23/eng/20230413
LC record available at https://lccn.loc.gov/2023001423
LC ebook record available at https://lccn.loc.gov/2023001424

Designed by Hilary Wacholz
Edited by Abby Huff

Cover and contributing artist: Scott Brown

THE FANTASTIC FREEWHEELER
and the Mega Bot Attack

A Graphic Novel

written by Molly Felder
illustrated by Rory Walker

STONE ARCH BOOKS
a capstone imprint

MEET THE FANTASTIC FREEWHEELER

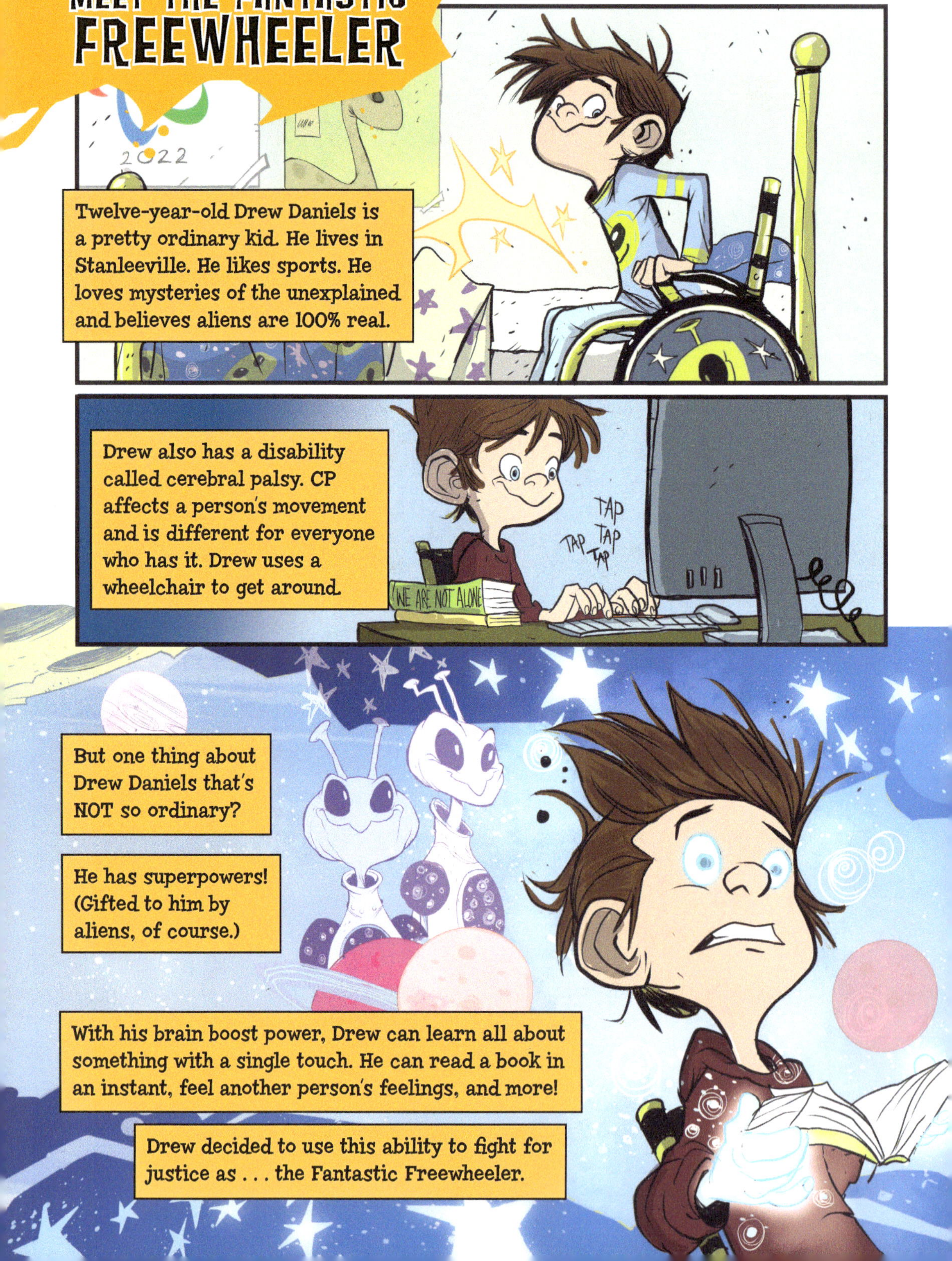

2022
Twelve-year-old Drew Daniels is a pretty ordinary kid. He lives in Stanleeville. He likes sports. He loves mysteries of the unexplained and believes aliens are 100% real.
Drew also has a disability called cerebral palsy. CP affects a person's movement and is different for everyone who has it. Drew uses a wheelchair to get around.
WE ARE NOT ALONE
TAP TAP TAP TAP
But one thing about Drew Daniels that's NOT so ordinary?
He has superpowers! (Gifted to him by aliens, of course.)
With his brain boost power, Drew can learn all about something with a single touch. He can read a book in an instant, feel another person's feelings, and more!
Drew decided to use this ability to fight for justice as . . . the Fantastic Freewheeler.

Every hero needs sidekicks, and Freewheeler can always count on his friends. There's Mikey Lang, who loves theater and being onstage.

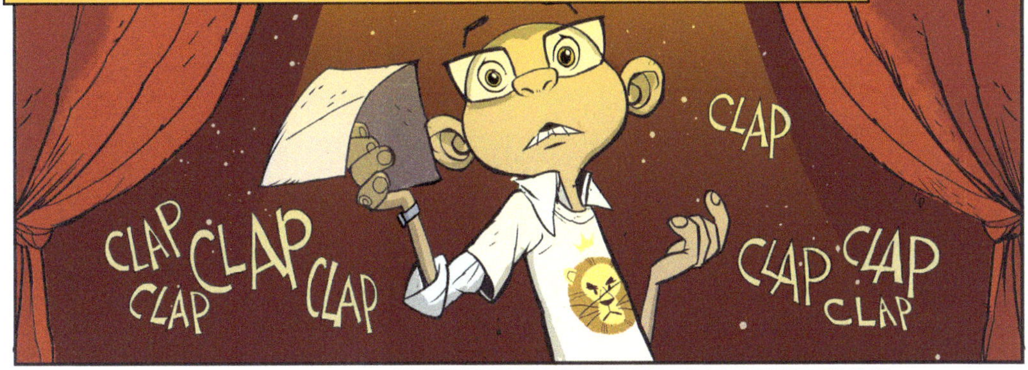
CLAP
CLAP
CLAP
CLAP
CLAP
CLAP
CLAP
CLAP

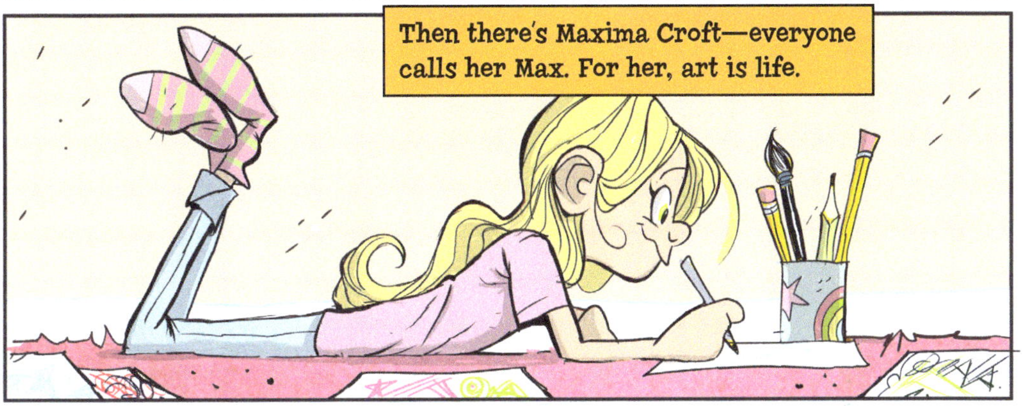

Then there's Maxima Croft—everyone calls her Max. For her, art is life.

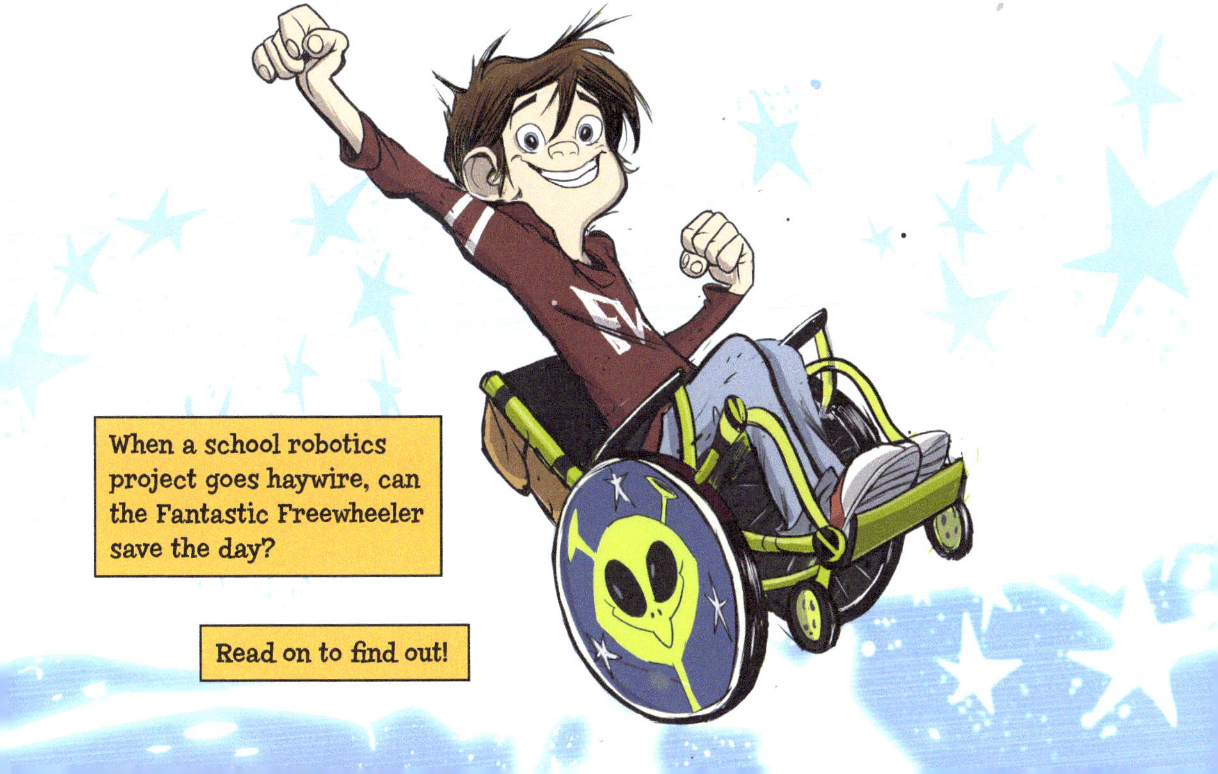

When a school robotics project goes haywire, can the Fantastic Freewheeler save the day?

Read on to find out!

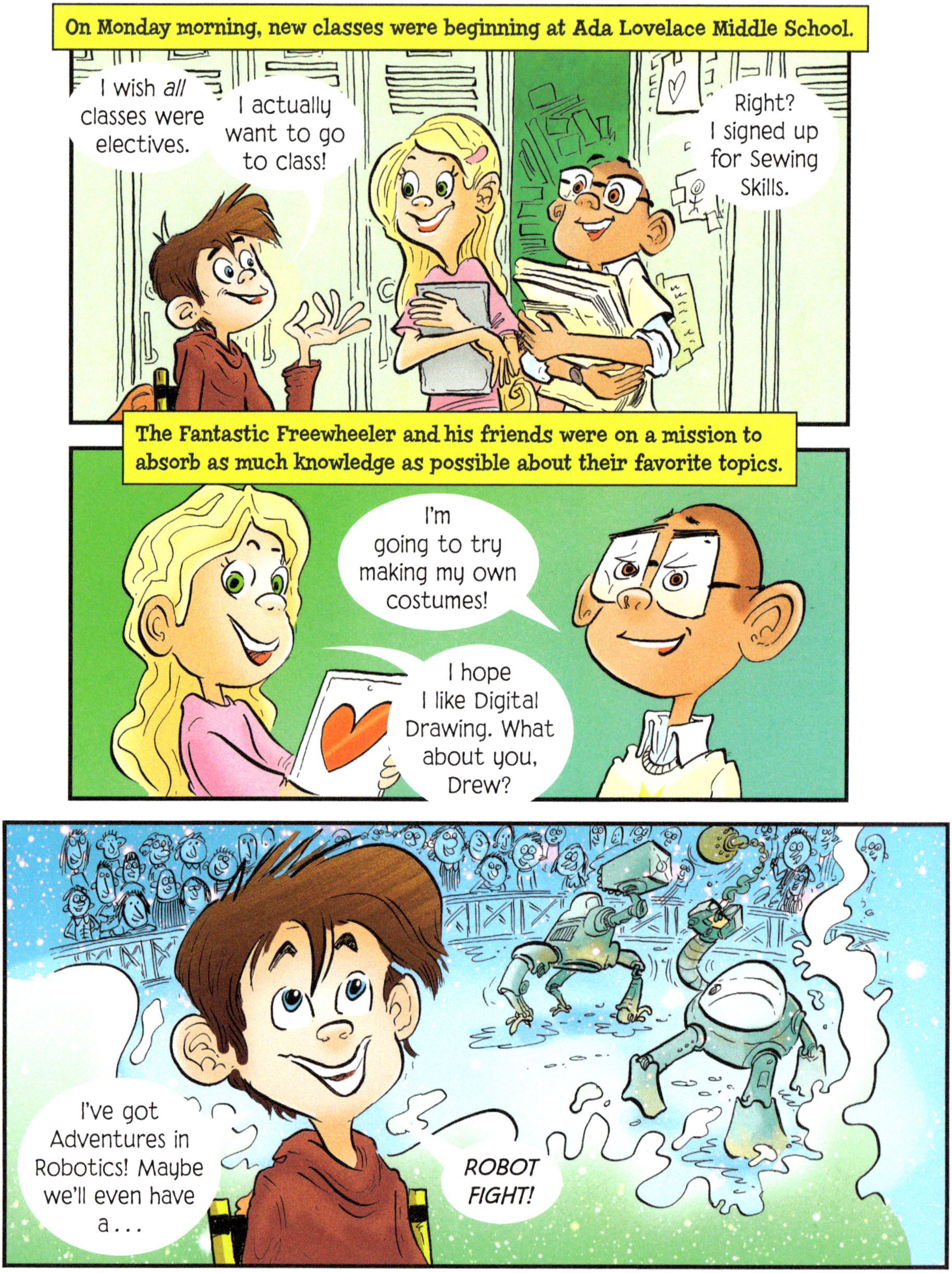
On Monday morning, new classes were beginning at Ada Lovelace Middle School.
I wish *all* classes were electives.
I actually want to go to class!
Right? I signed up for Sewing Skills.
The Fantastic Freewheeler and his friends were on a mission to absorb as much knowledge as possible about their favorite topics.
I'm going to try making my own costumes!
I hope I like Digital Drawing. What about you, Drew?
I've got Adventures in Robotics! Maybe we'll even have a . . .
ROBOT FIGHT!

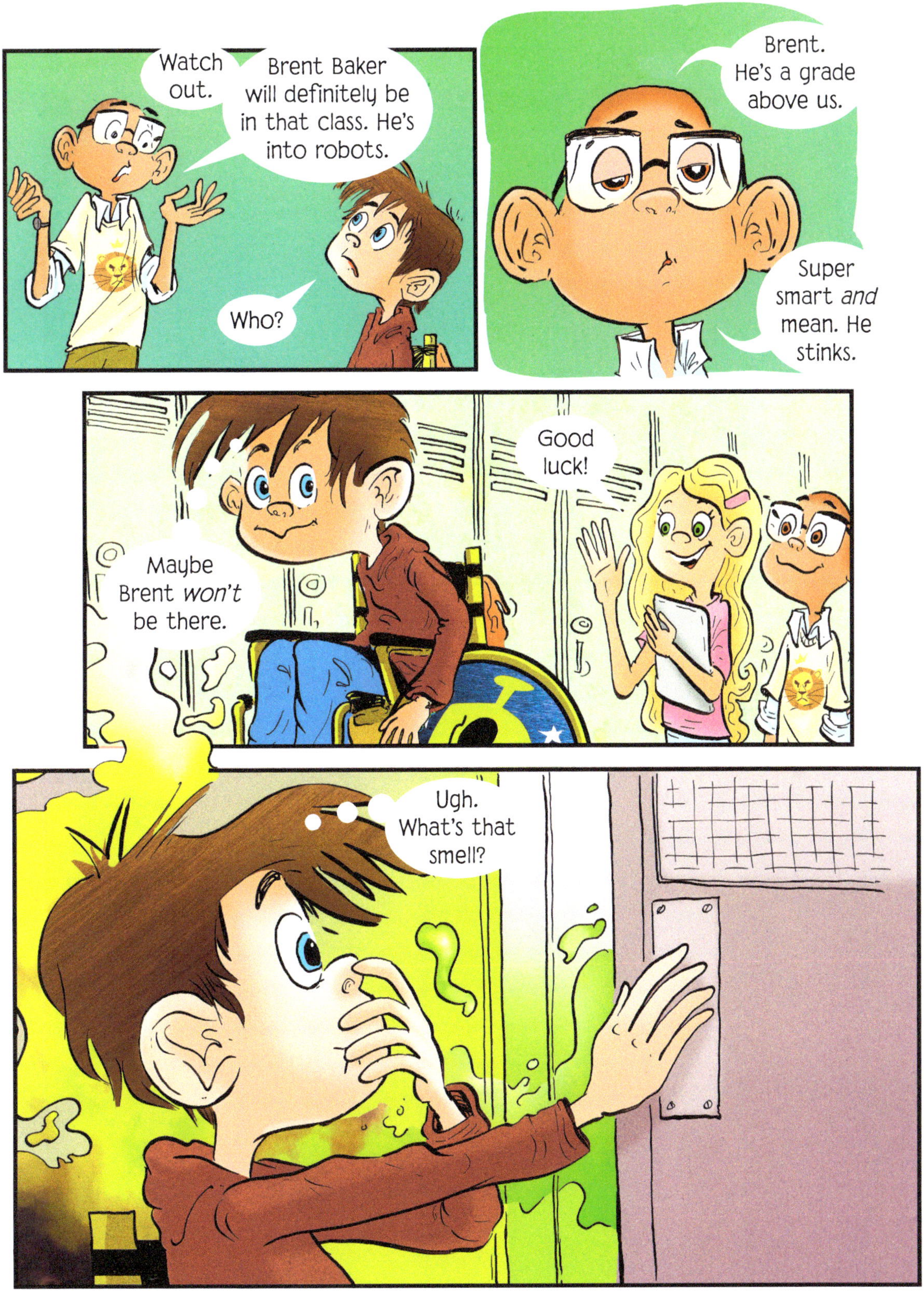
Watch out.
Brent Baker will definitely be in that class. He's into robots.
Who?
Brent. He's a grade above us.
Super smart *and* mean. He stinks.
Good luck!
Maybe Brent *won't* be there.
Ugh. What's that smell?

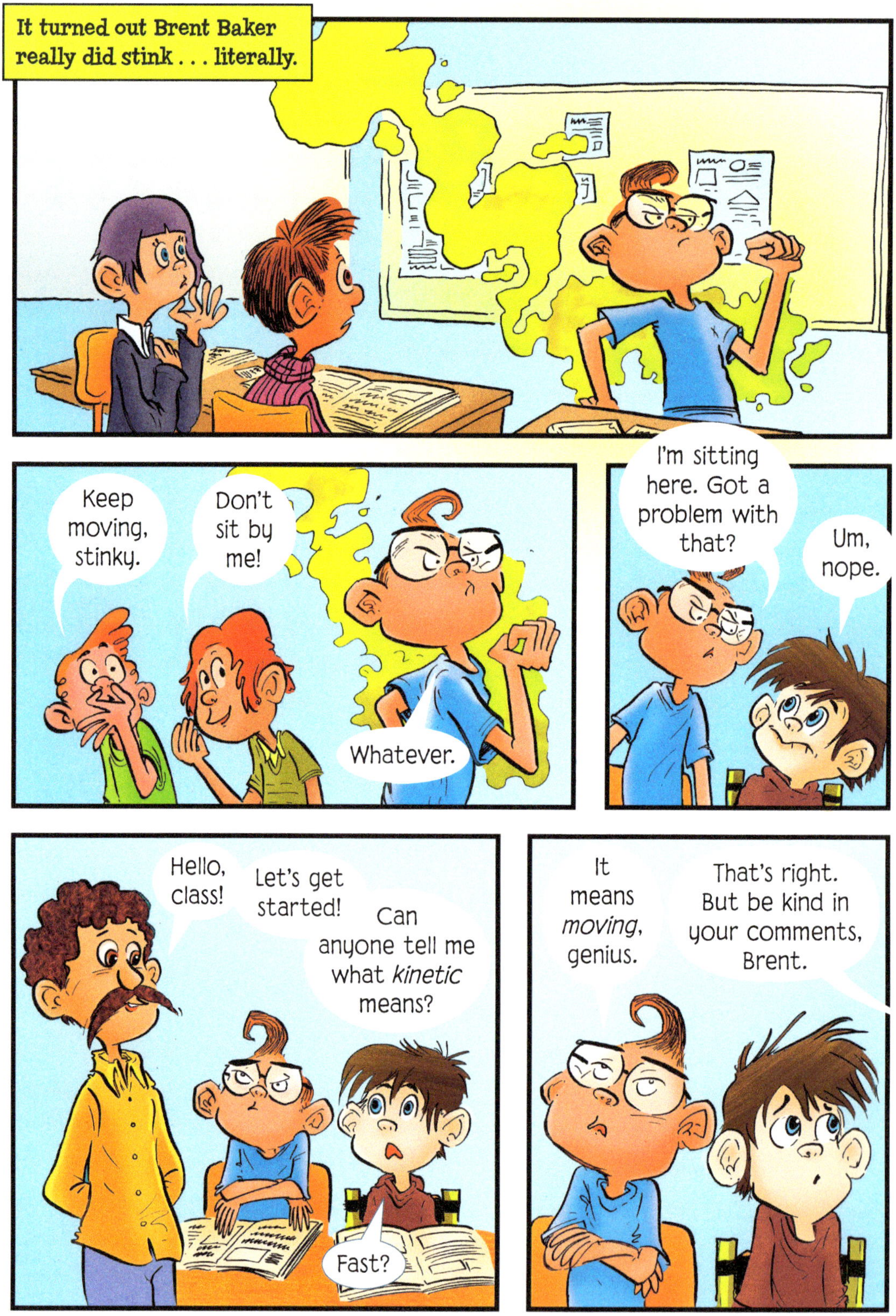
It turned out Brent Baker really did stink . . . literally.
Keep moving, stinky.
Don't sit by me!
Whatever.
I'm sitting here. Got a problem with that?
Um, nope.
Hello, class!
Let's get started!
Can anyone tell me what *kinetic* means?
Fast?
It means *moving*, genius.
That's right. But be kind in your comments, Brent.

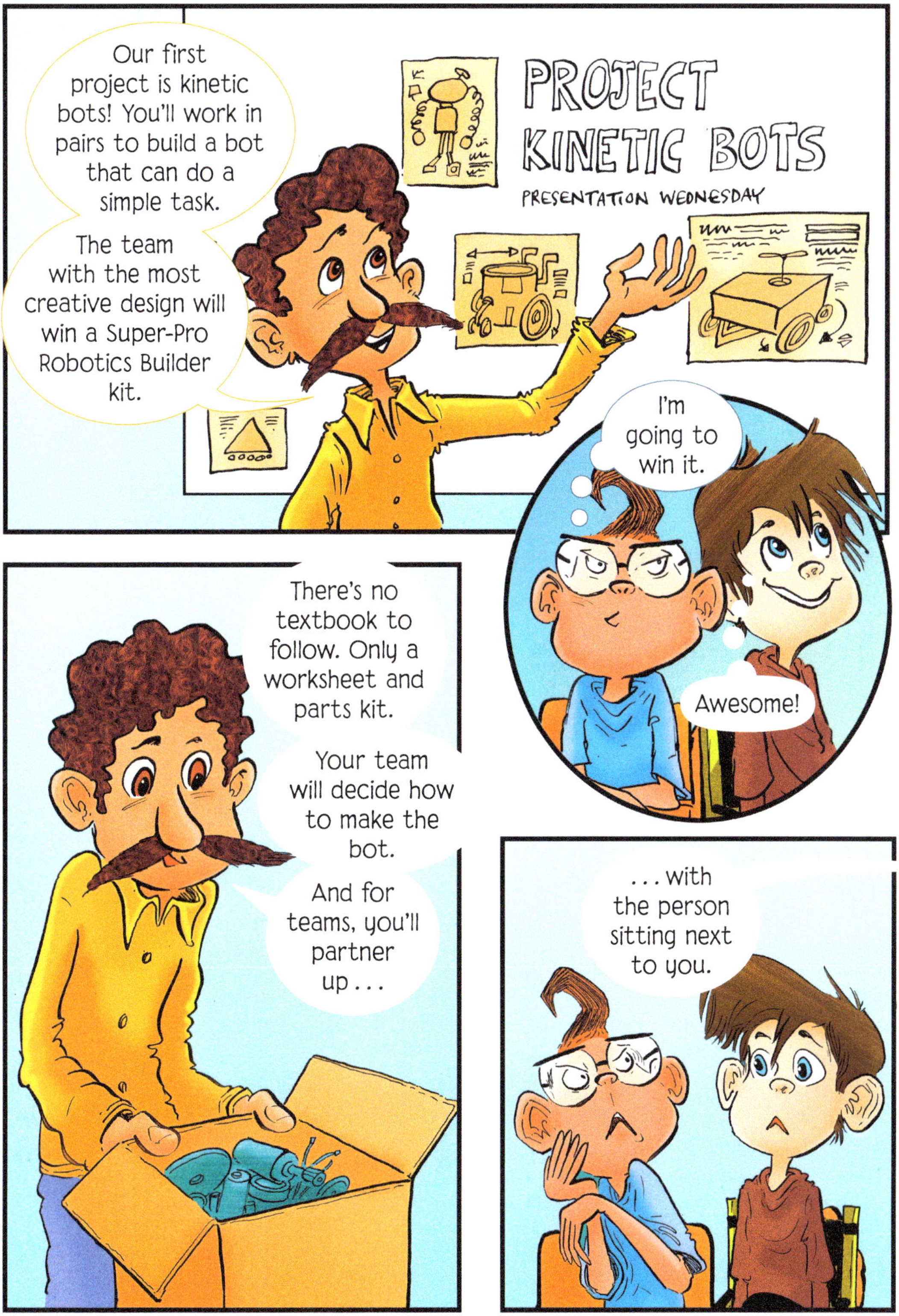
Our first project is kinetic bots! You'll work in pairs to build a bot that can do a simple task.
The team with the most creative design will win a Super-Pro Robotics Builder kit.
PROJECT KINETIC BOTS
PRESENTATION WEDNESDAY
I'm going to win it.
Awesome!
There's no textbook to follow. Only a worksheet and parts kit.
Your team will decide how to make the bot.
And for teams, you'll partner up . . .
. . . with the person sitting next to you.

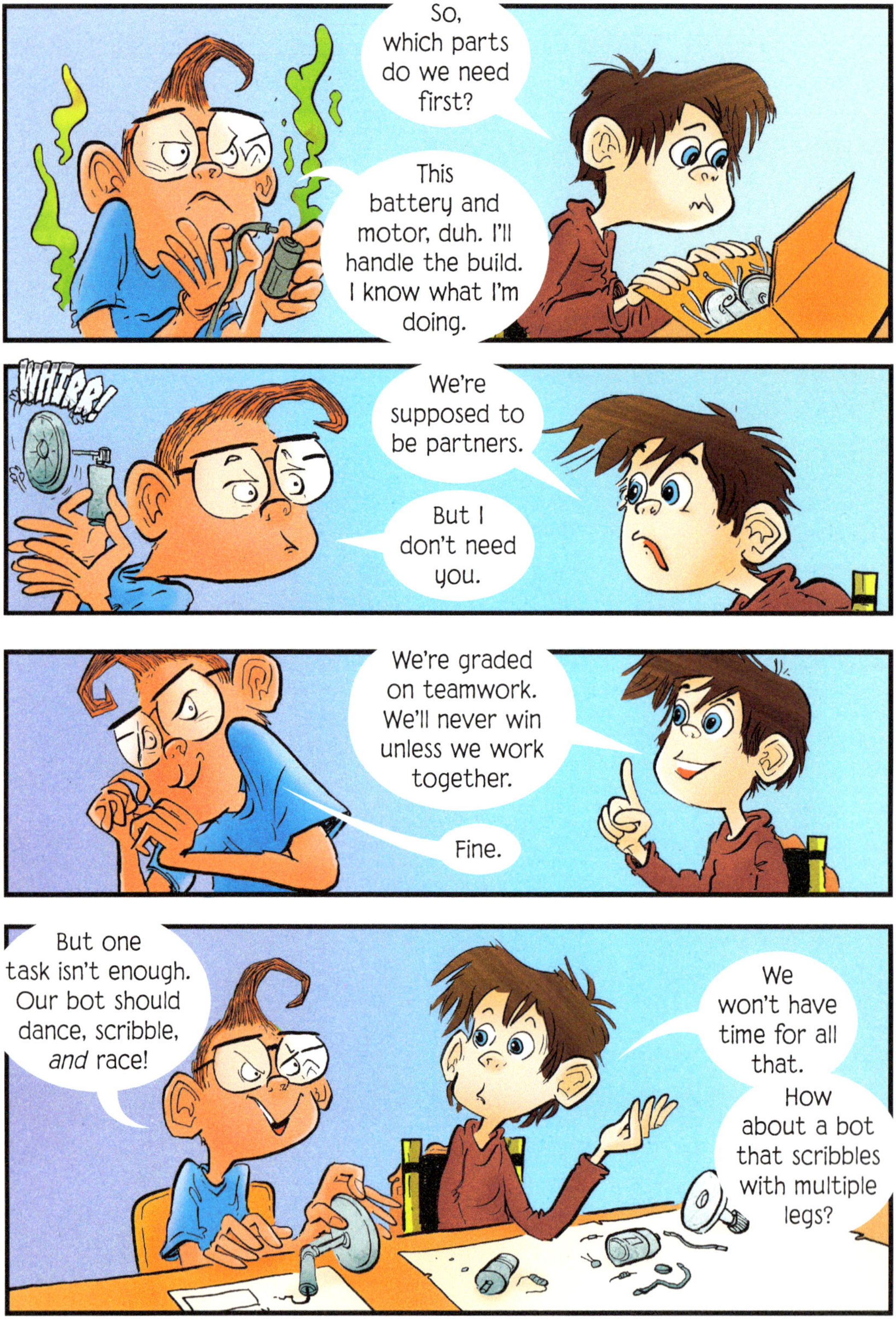

So, which parts do we need first?
This battery and motor, duh. I'll handle the build. I know what I'm doing.
WHIRR!
We're supposed to be partners.
But I don't need you.
We're graded on teamwork. We'll never win unless we work together.
Fine.
But one task isn't enough. Our bot should dance, scribble, *and* race!
We won't have time for all that.
How about a bot that scribbles with multiple legs?

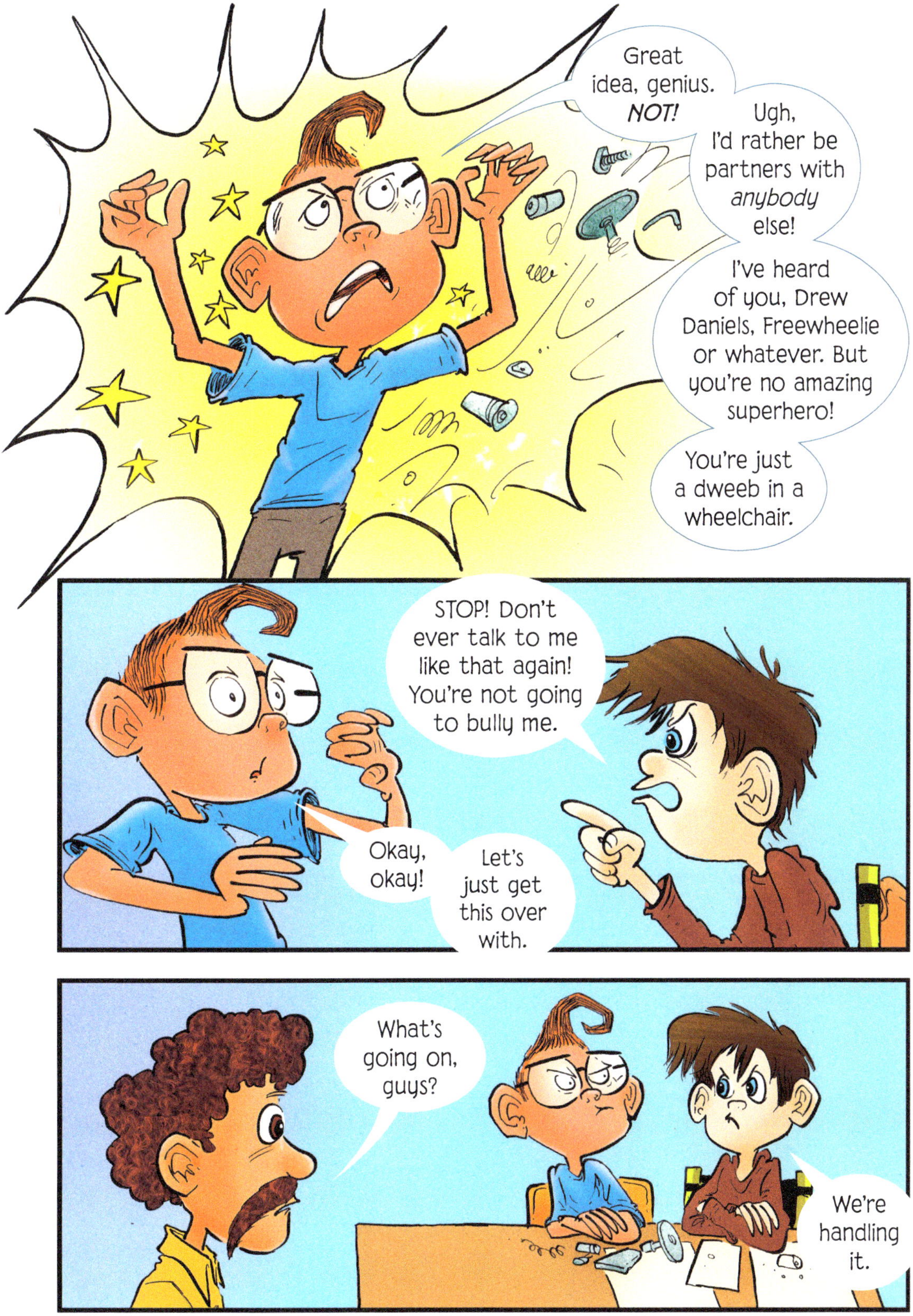
Great idea, genius. *NOT!*
Ugh, I'd rather be partners with *anybody* else!
I've heard of you, Drew Daniels, Freewheelie or whatever. But you're no amazing superhero!
You're just a dweeb in a wheelchair.
STOP! Don't ever talk to me like that again! You're not going to bully me.
Okay, okay!
Let's just get this over with.
What's going on, guys?
We're handling it.

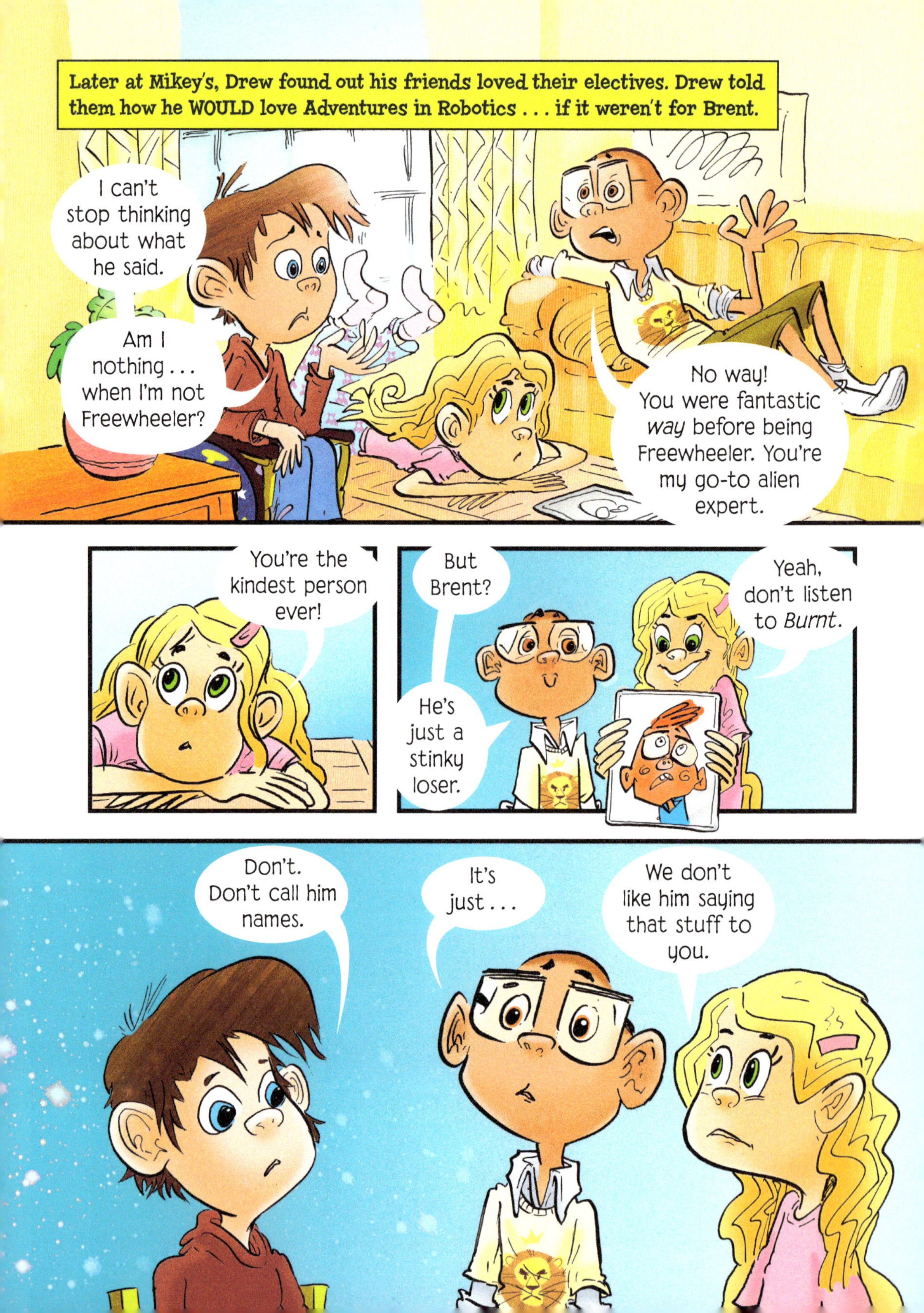
Later at Mikey's, Drew found out his friends loved their electives. Drew told them how he WOULD love Adventures in Robotics . . . if it weren't for Brent.
I can't stop thinking about what he said.
Am I nothing . . . when I'm not Freewheeler?
No way! You were fantastic *way* before being Freewheeler. You're my go-to alien expert.
You're the kindest person ever!
But Brent?
He's just a stinky loser.
Yeah, don't listen to *Burnt*.
Don't. Don't call him names.
It's just . . .
We don't like him saying that stuff to you.

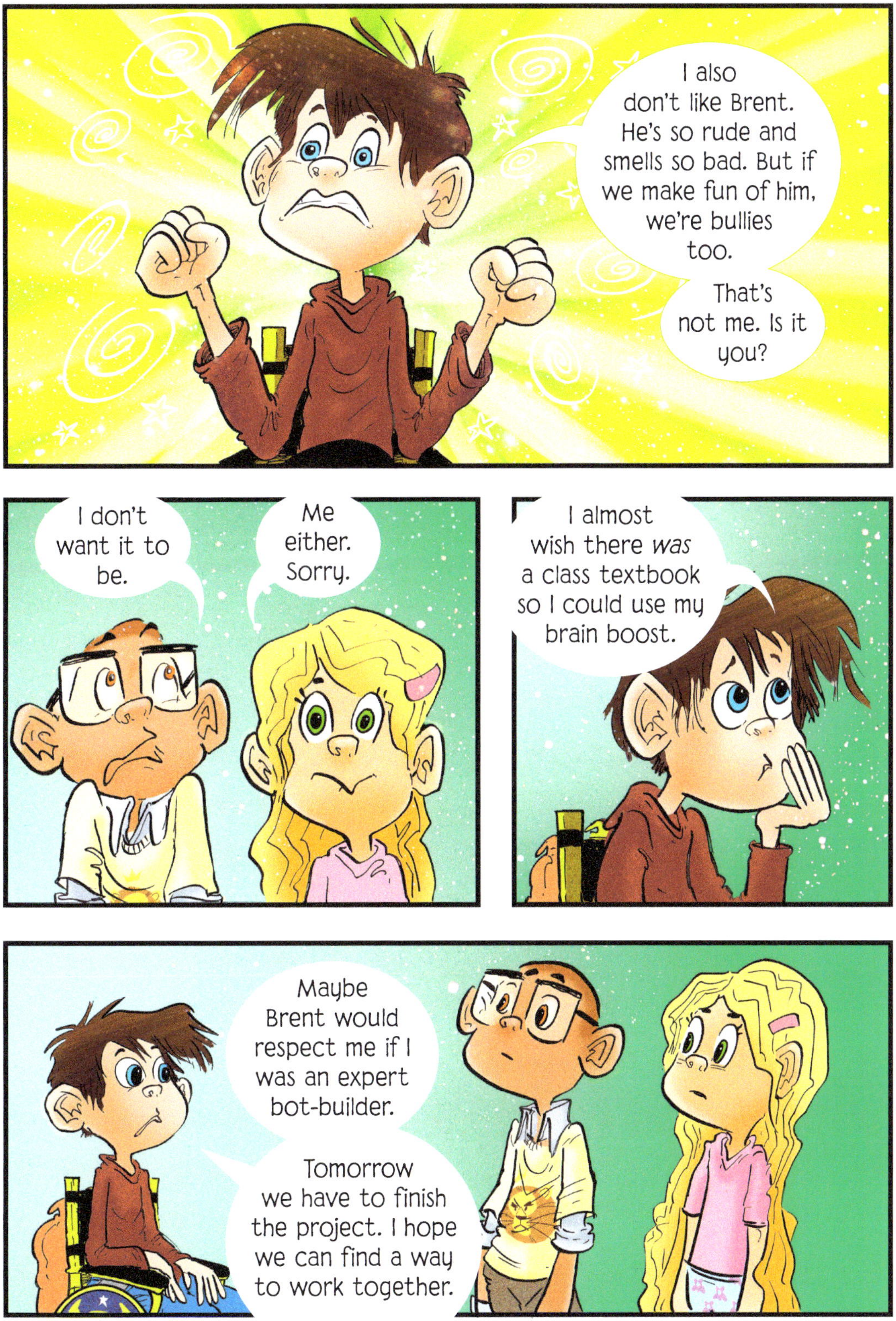
I also don't like Brent. He's so rude and smells so bad. But if we make fun of him, we're bullies too.
That's not me. Is it you?
I don't want it to be.
Me either. Sorry.
I almost wish there *was* a class textbook so I could use my brain boost.
Maybe Brent would respect me if I was an expert bot-builder.
Tomorrow we have to finish the project. I hope we can find a way to work together.

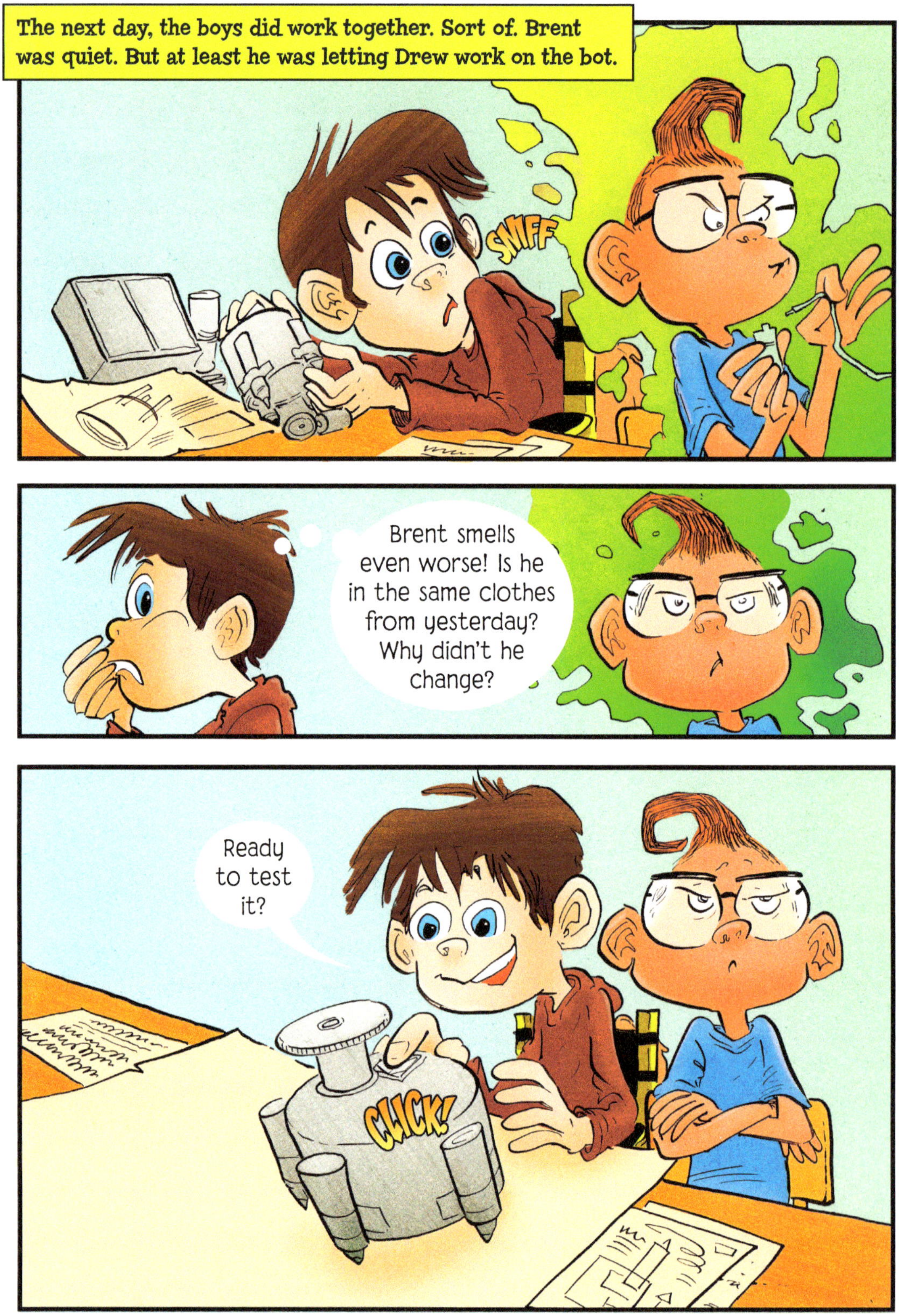
The next day, the boys did work together. Sort of. Brent was quiet. But at least he was letting Drew work on the bot.
SNIFF
Brent smells even worse! Is he in the same clothes from yesterday? Why didn't he change?
Ready to test it?
CLICK!

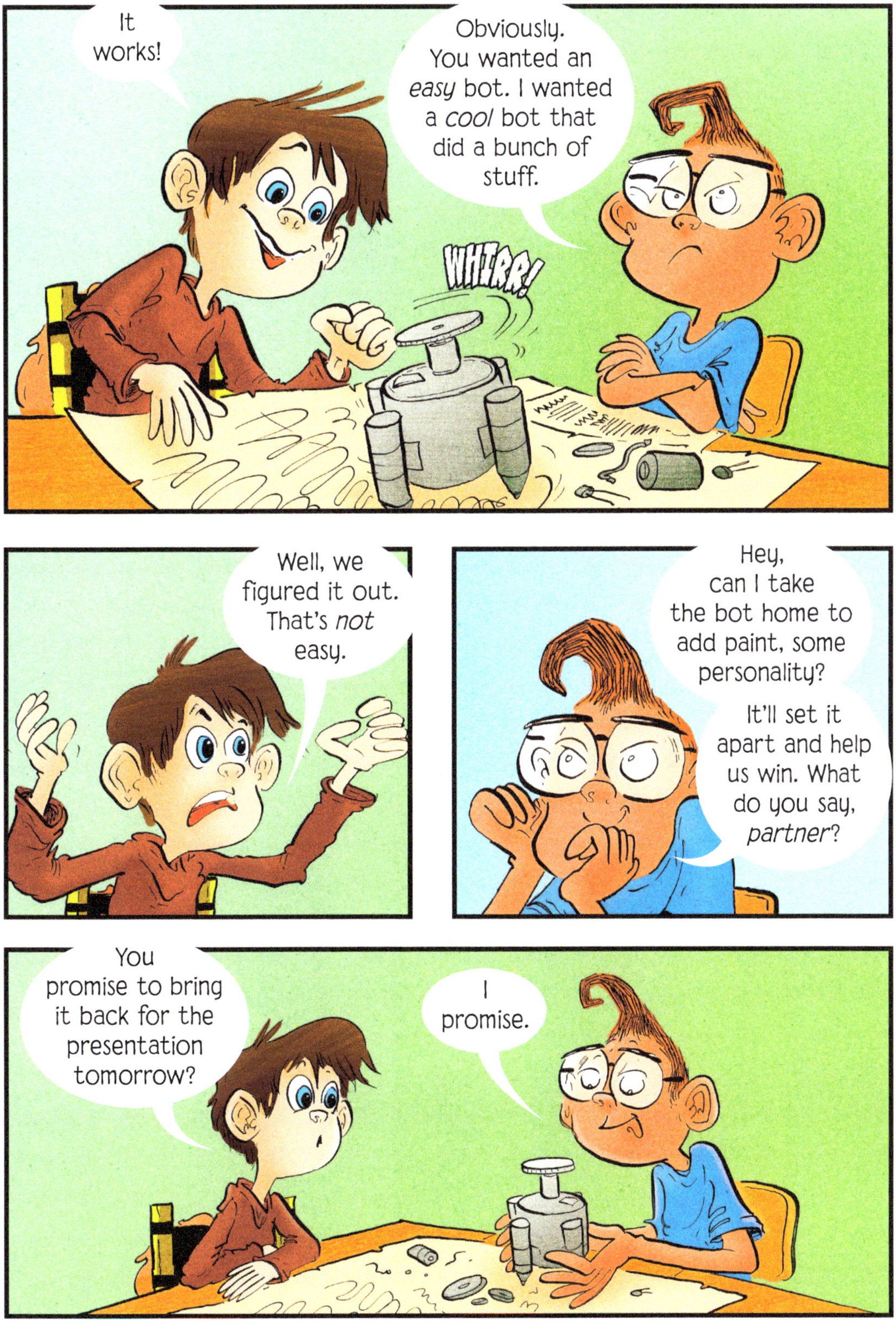
It works!
Obviously. You wanted an *easy* bot. I wanted a *cool* bot that did a bunch of stuff.
WHIRR!
Well, we figured it out. That's *not* easy.
Hey, can I take the bot home to add paint, some personality?
It'll set it apart and help us win. What do you say, *partner*?
You promise to bring it back for the presentation tomorrow?
I promise.

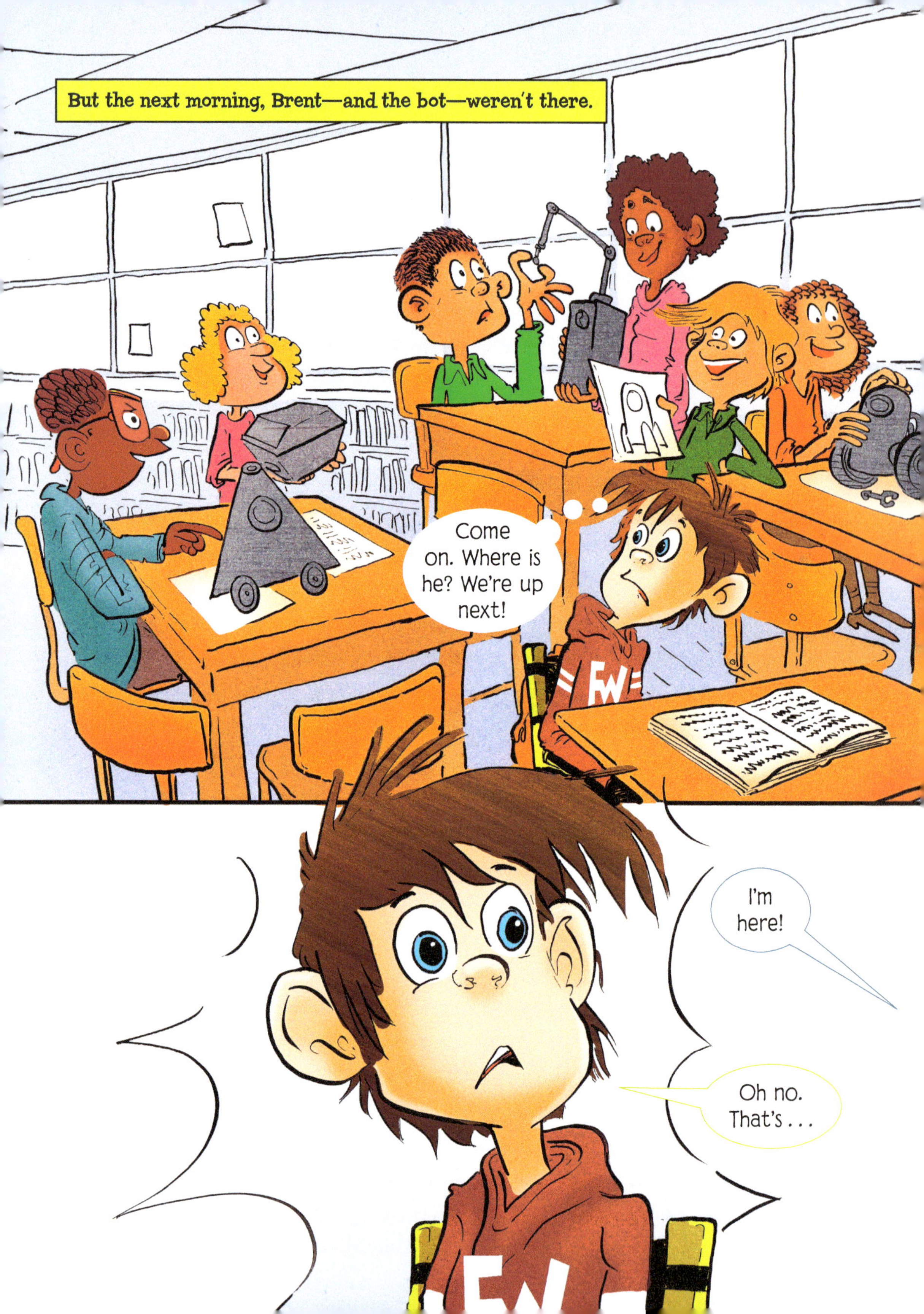

But the next morning, Brent—and the bot—weren't there.
Come on. Where is he? We're up next!
I'm here!
Oh no. That's . . .

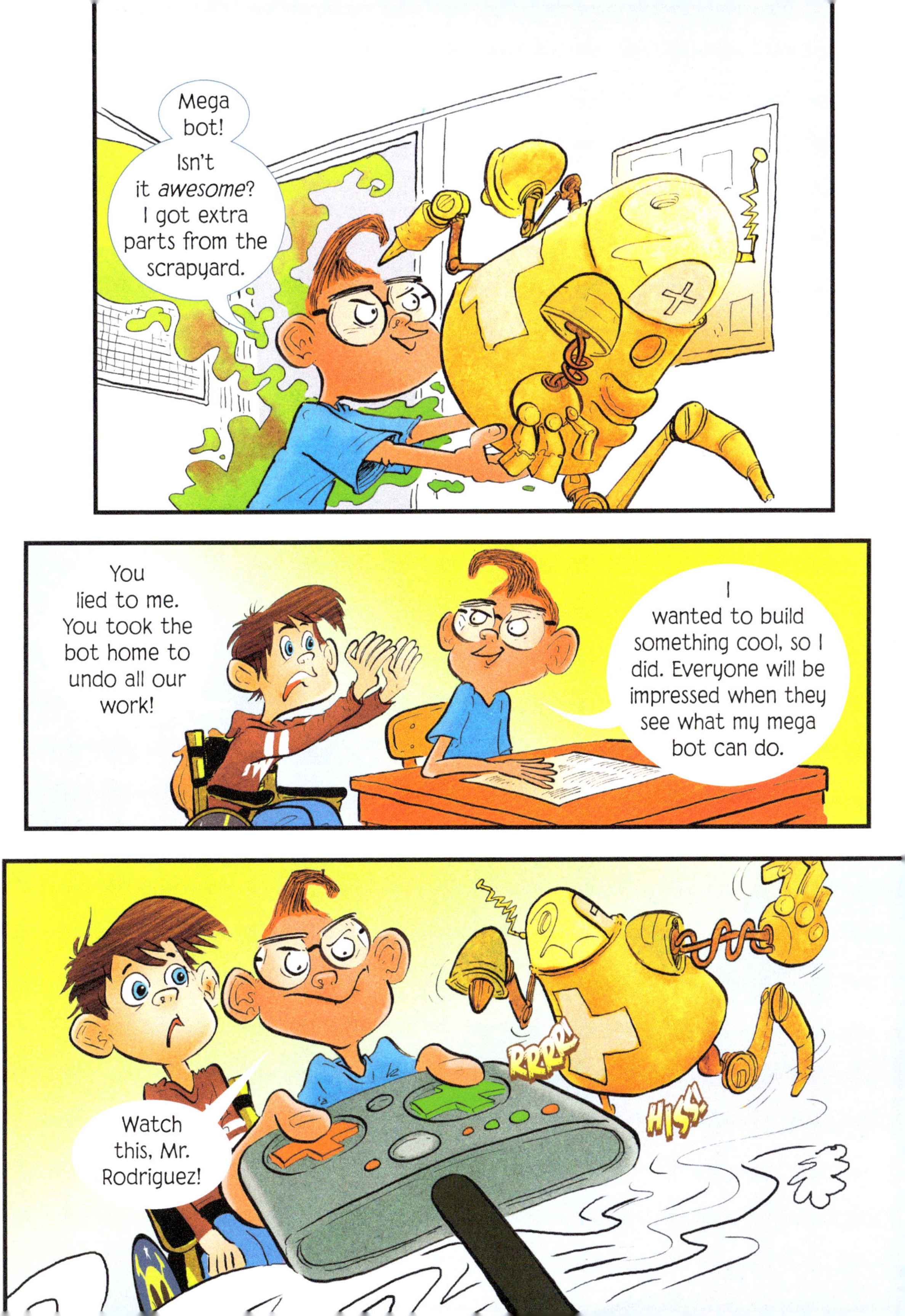
Mega bot!
Isn't it *awesome*? I got extra parts from the scrapyard.
You lied to me. You took the bot home to undo all our work!
I wanted to build something cool, so I did. Everyone will be impressed when they see what my mega bot can do.
Watch this, Mr. Rodriguez!
RRRR!
HISS!

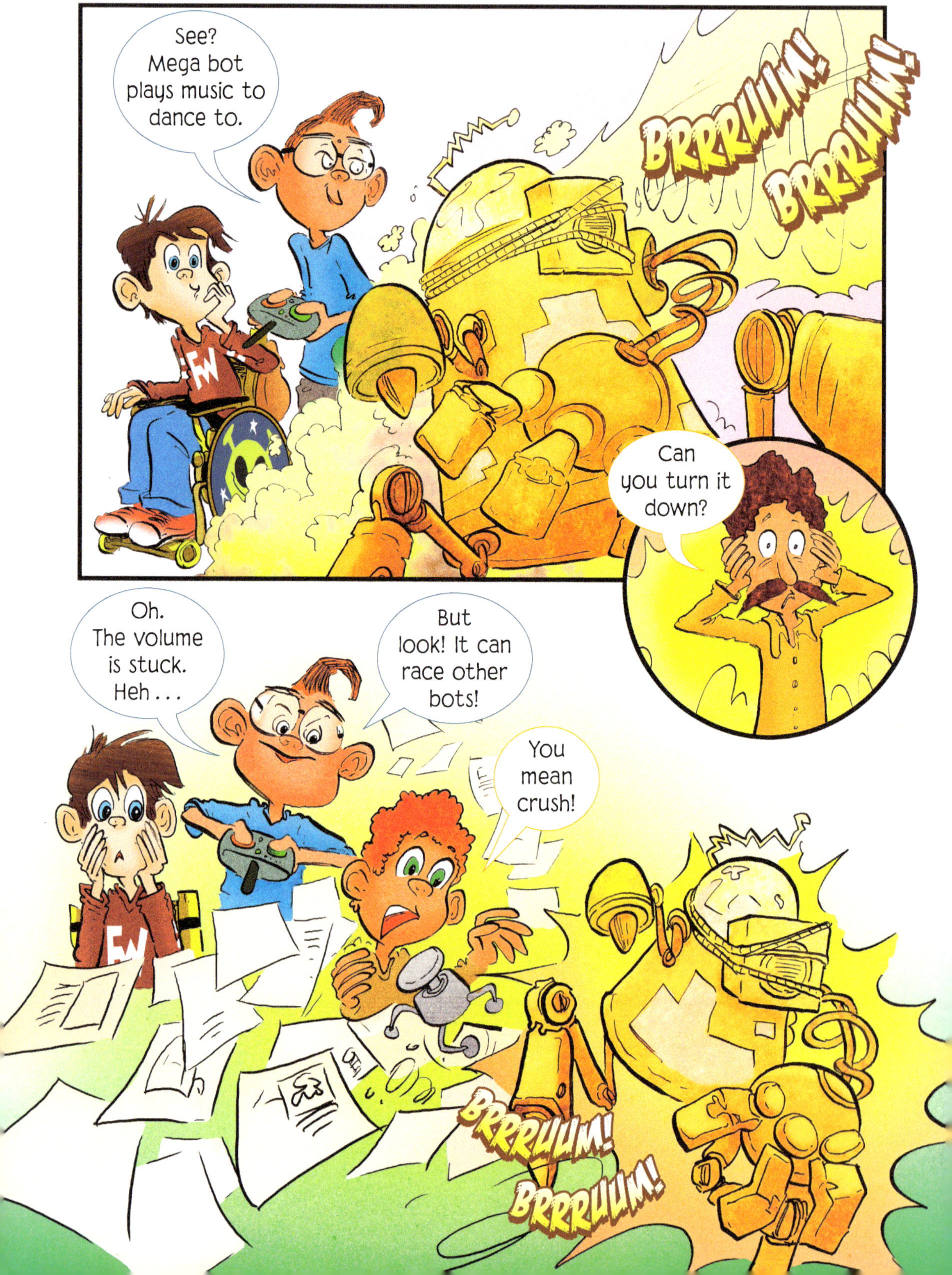
See? Mega bot plays music to dance to.
BRRRUUM! BRRRUUM!
Can you turn it down?
Oh. The volume is stuck. Heh . . .
But look! It can race other bots!
You mean crush!
BRRRUUM! BRRRUUM!

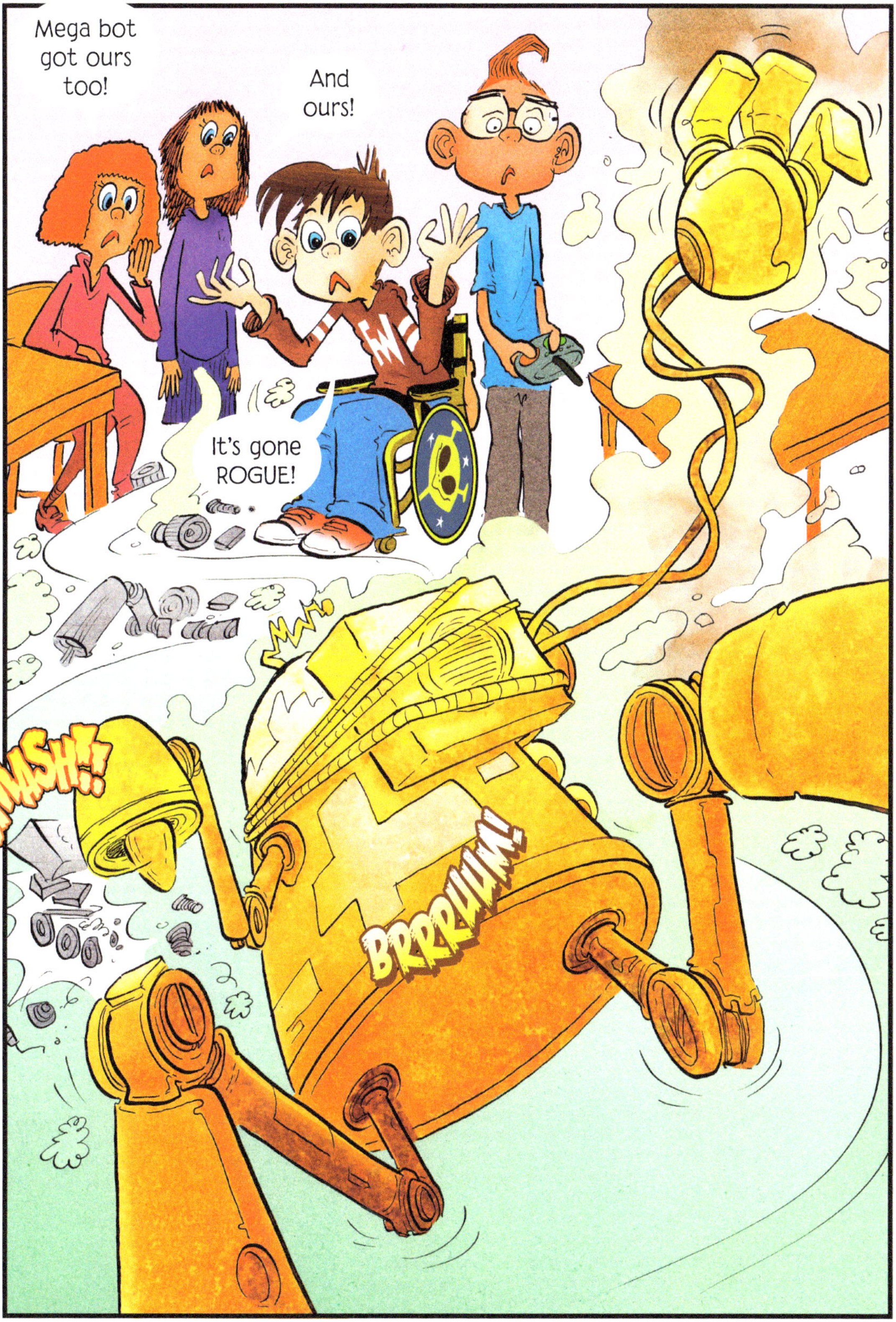
Mega bot got ours too!
And ours!
It's gone ROGUE!
SMASH!!
BRRRUUM!

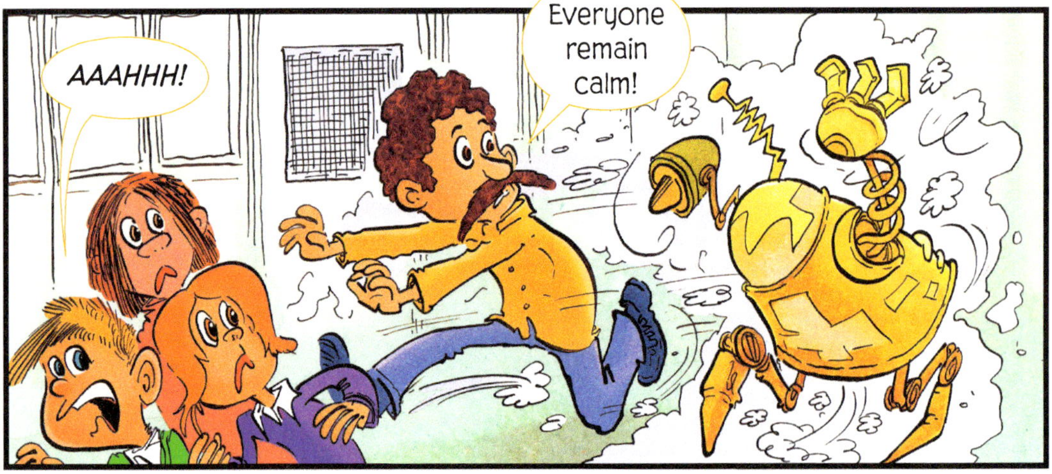
AAAHHH!
Everyone remain calm!

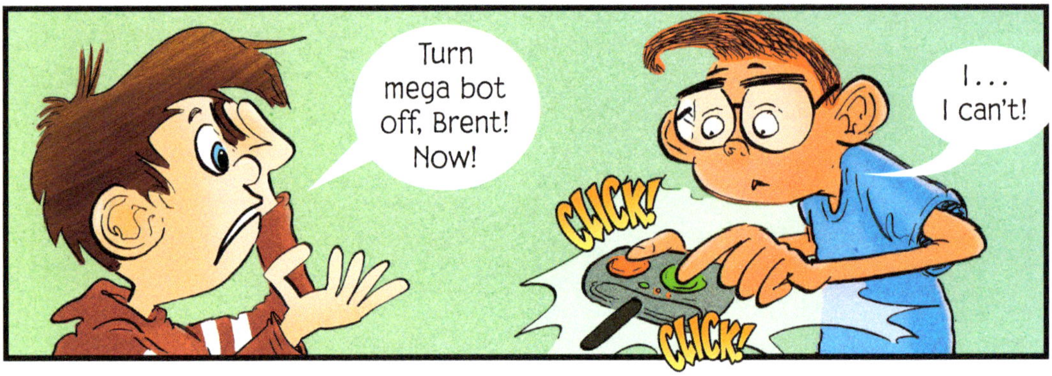
Turn mega bot off, Brent! Now!
CLICK!
CLICK!
I . . . I can't!

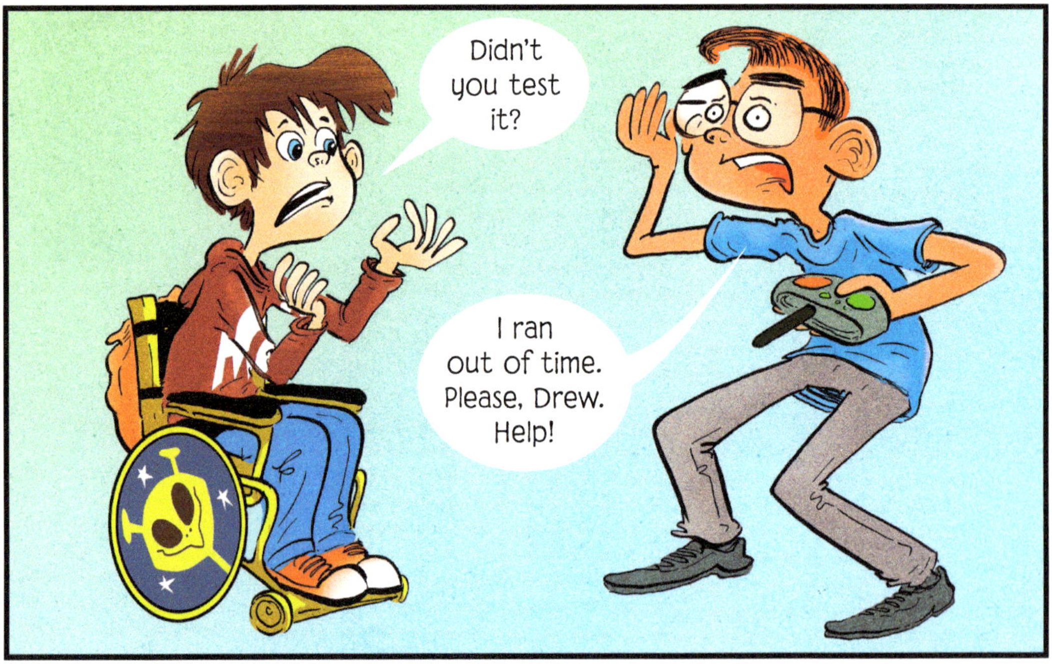
Didn't you test it?
I ran out of time. Please, Drew. Help!

Part of Drew didn't want to do anything. But as a superhero, he'd promised to help whoever needed it. Right now, he had a job to do.

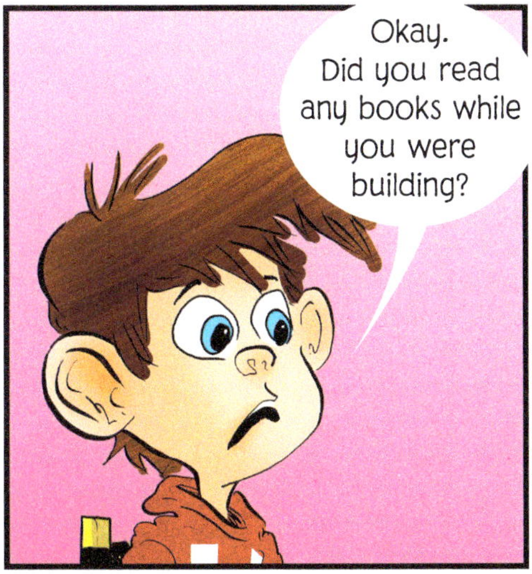
Okay. Did you read any books while you were building?

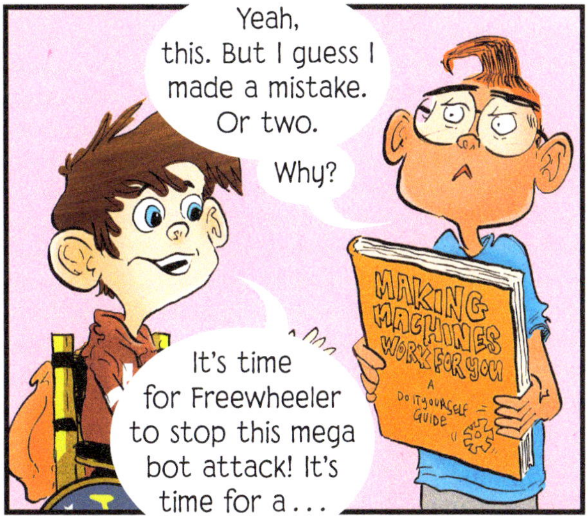
Yeah, this. But I guess I made a mistake. Or two.
Why?
MAKING MACHINES WORK FOR YOU
A DO IT YOURSELF GUIDE
It's time for Freewheeler to stop this mega bot attack! It's time for a . . .

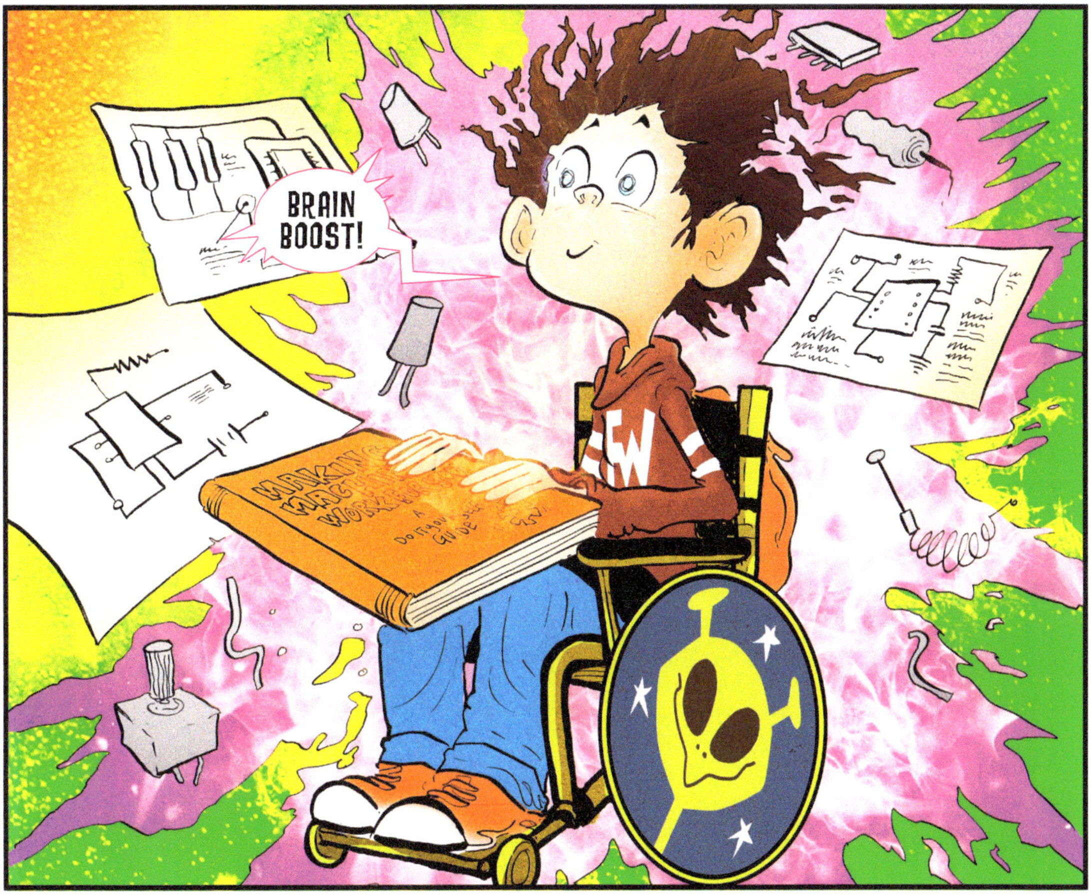
BRAIN BOOST!

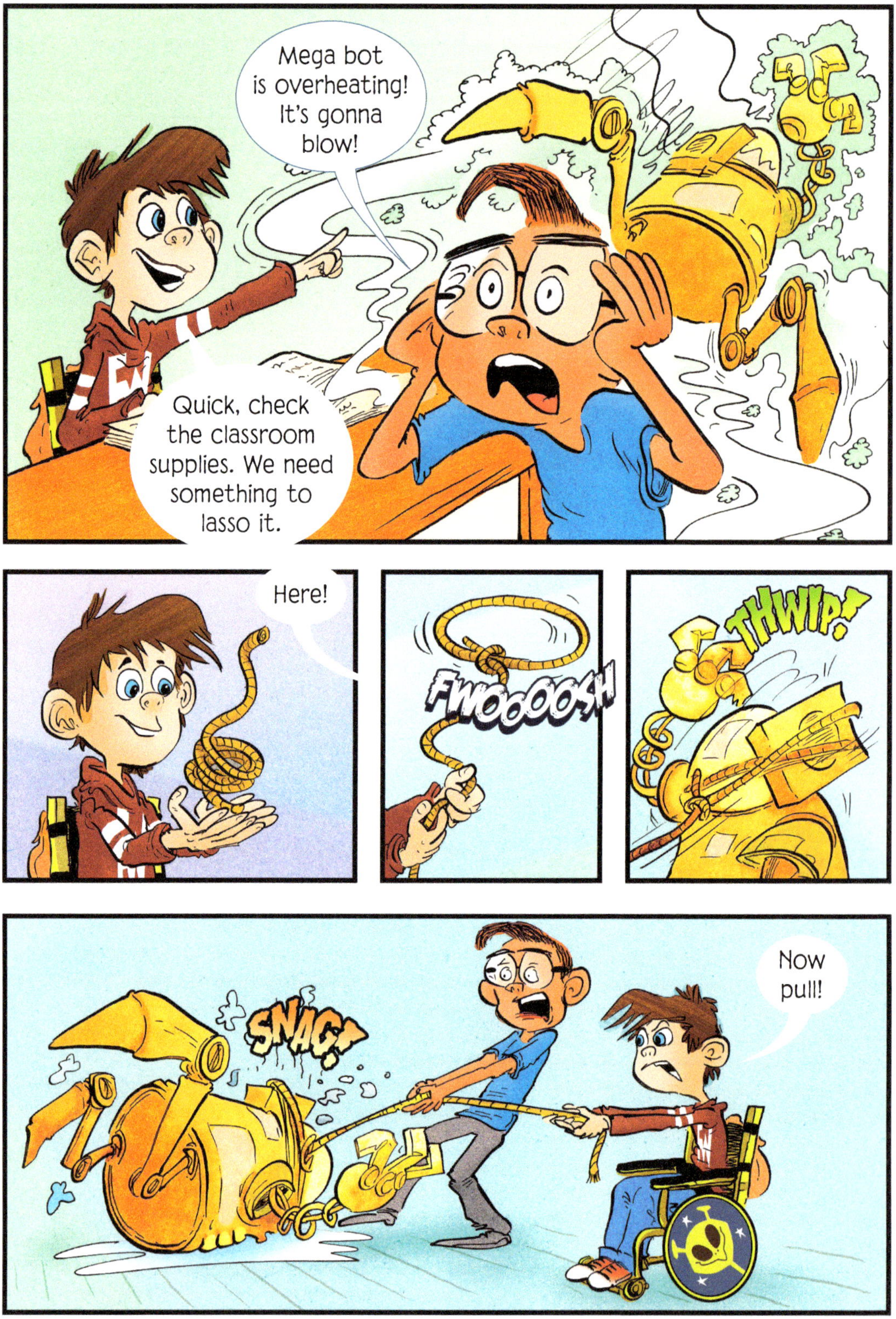
Mega bot is overheating! It's gonna blow!
Quick, check the classroom supplies. We need something to lasso it.
Here!
FWOOOOSH
THWIP!
SNAG!
Now pull!

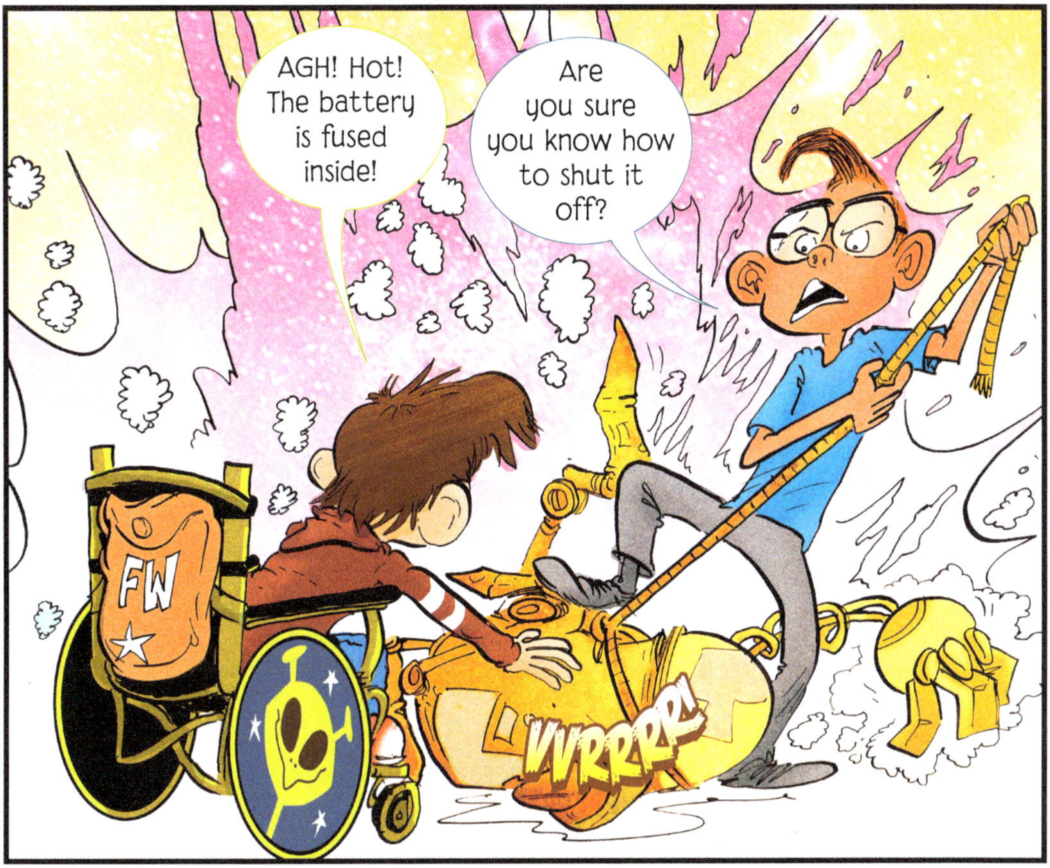
AGH! Hot! The battery is fused inside!
Are you sure you know how to shut it off?
VVRRRR!

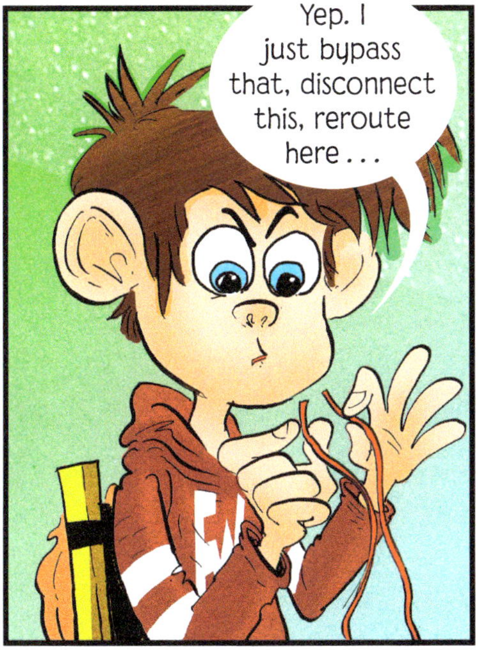
Yep. I just bypass that, disconnect this, reroute here . . .

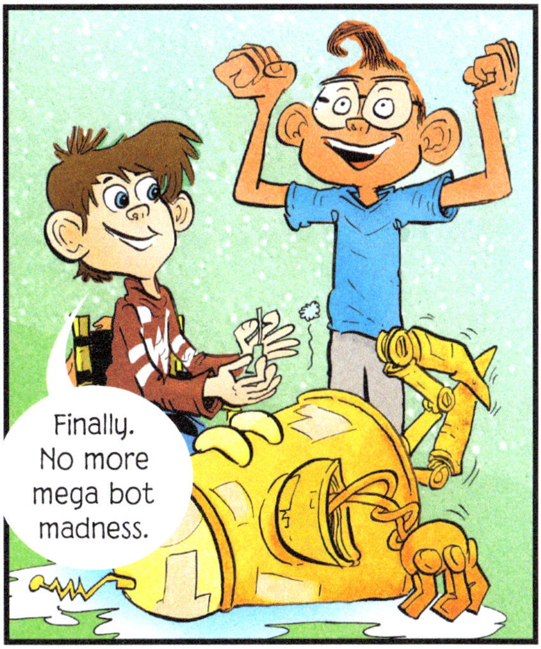
Finally. No more mega bot madness.

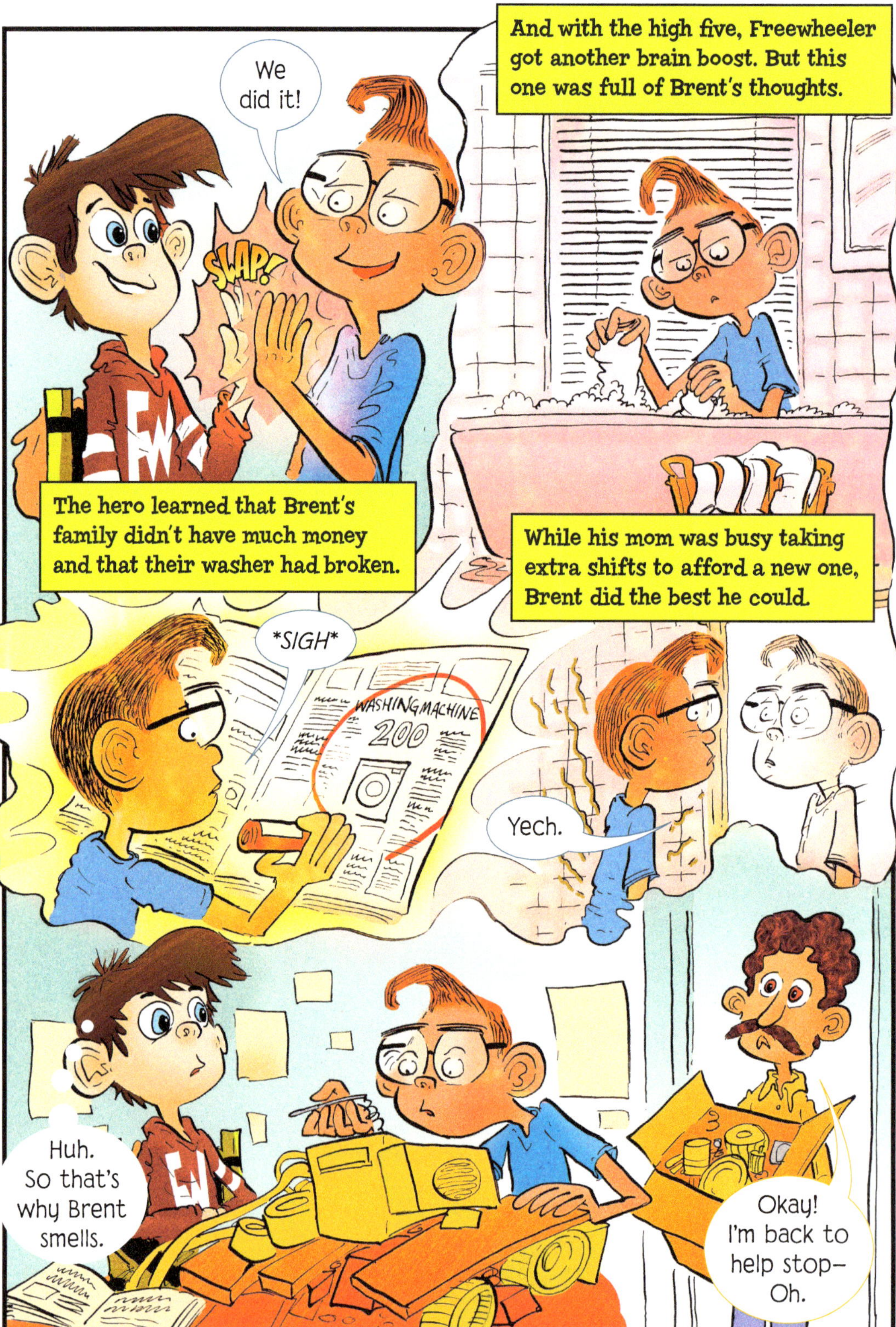
We did it!
SLAP!
And with the high five, Freewheeler got another brain boost. But this one was full of Brent's thoughts.
The hero learned that Brent's family didn't have much money and that their washer had broken.
While his mom was busy taking extra shifts to afford a new one, Brent did the best he could.
SIGH
WASHING MACHINE
200
Yech.
Huh. So that's why Brent smells.
Okay! I'm back to help stop— Oh.

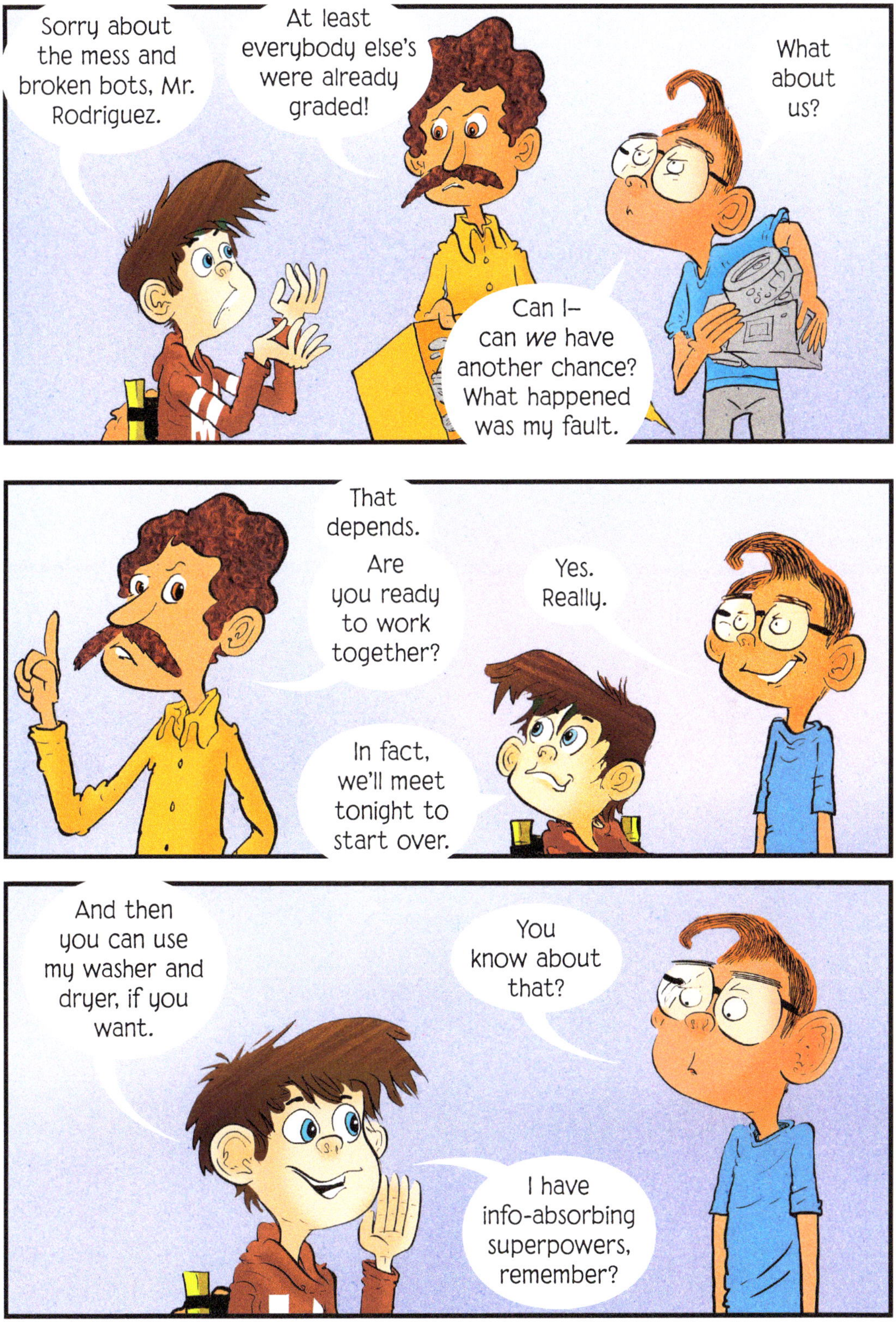
Sorry about the mess and broken bots, Mr. Rodriguez.
At least everybody else's were already graded!
What about us?
Can I– can *we* have another chance? What happened was my fault.
That depends.
Are you ready to work together?
Yes. Really.
In fact, we'll meet tonight to start over.
And then you can use my washer and dryer, if you want.
You know about that?
I have info-absorbing superpowers, remember?

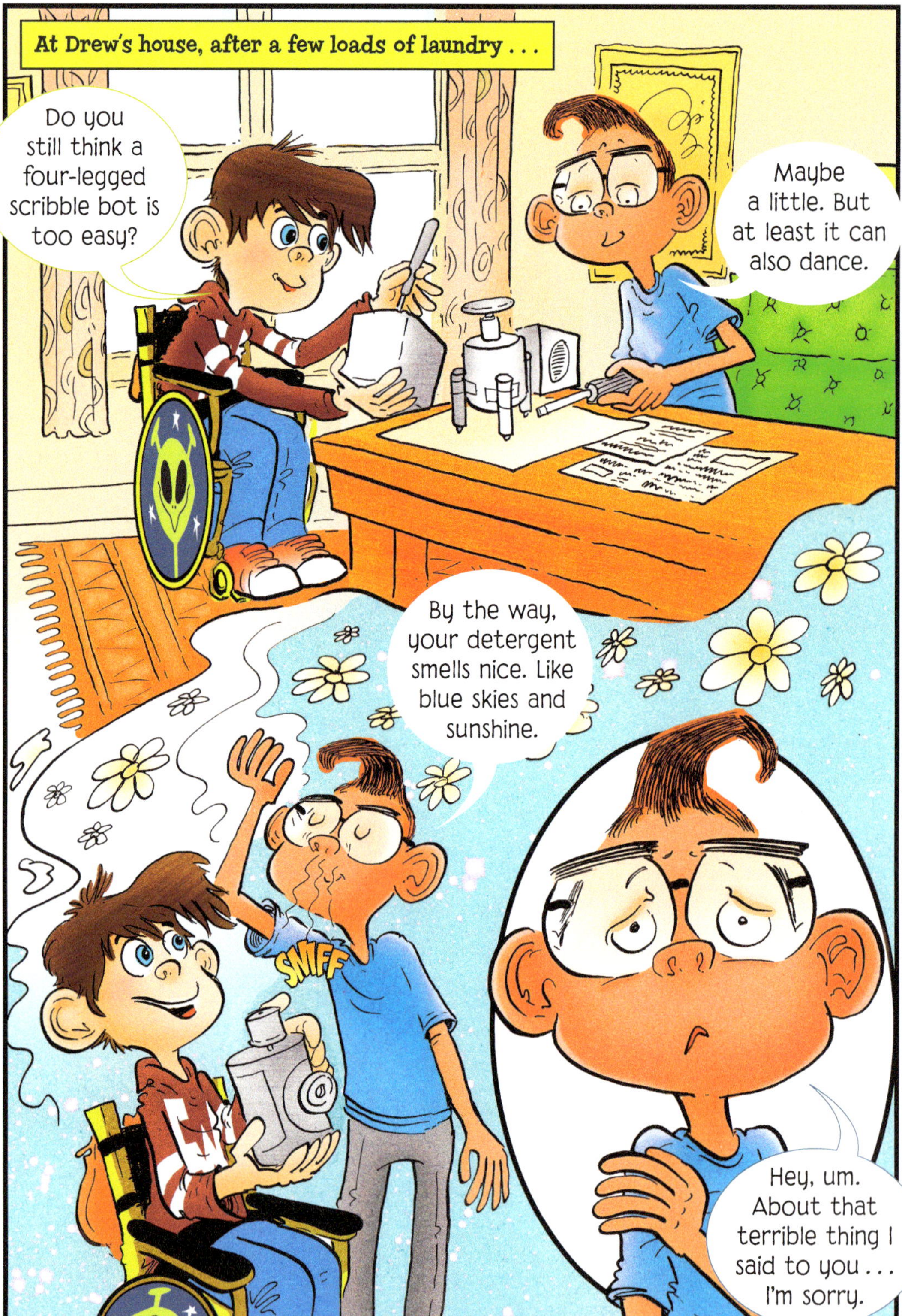
At Drew's house, after a few loads of laundry . . .
Do you still think a four-legged scribble bot is too easy?
Maybe a little. But at least it can also dance.
By the way, your detergent smells nice. Like blue skies and sunshine.
SNIFF
Hey, um. About that terrible thing I said to you . . . I'm sorry.

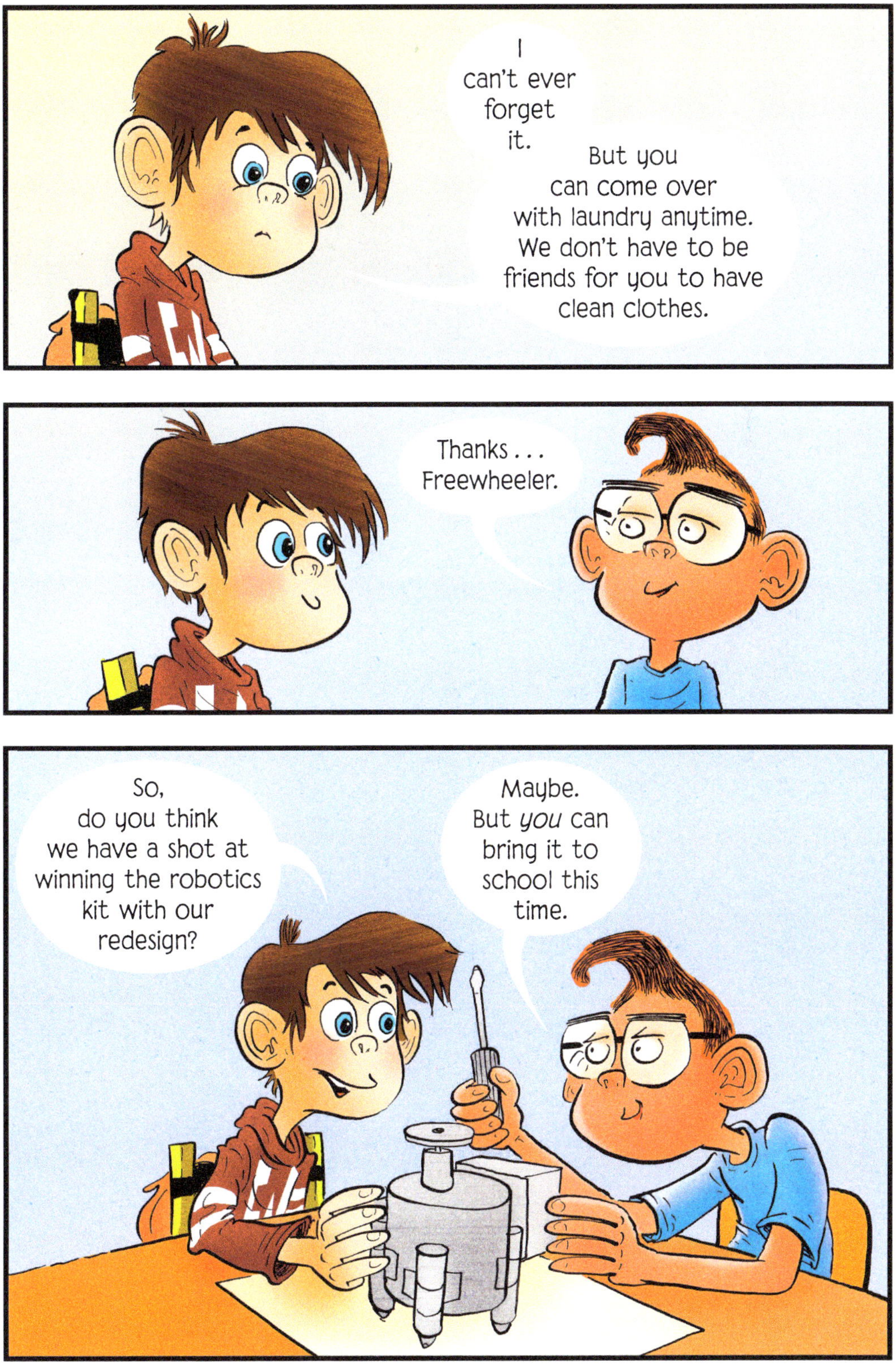
I can't ever forget it.
But you can come over with laundry anytime. We don't have to be friends for you to have clean clothes.
Thanks . . . Freewheeler.
So, do you think we have a shot at winning the robotics kit with our redesign?
Maybe. But *you* can bring it to school this time.

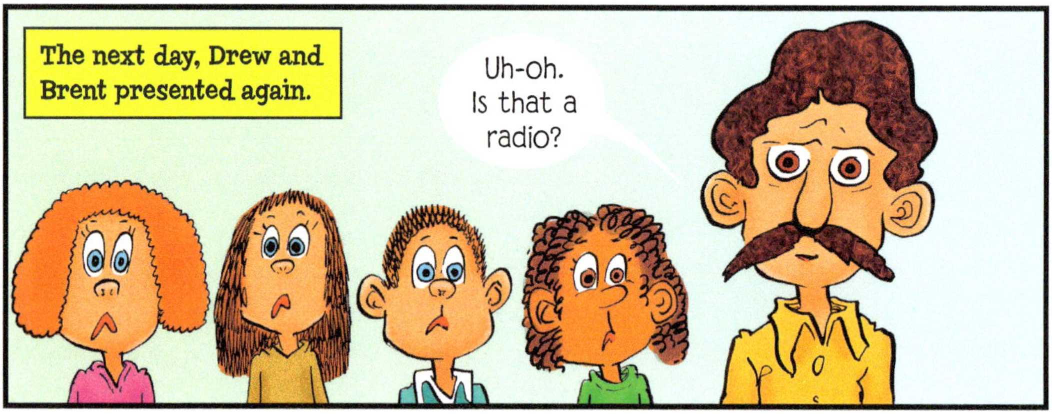
The next day, Drew and Brent presented again.
Uh-oh. Is that a radio?

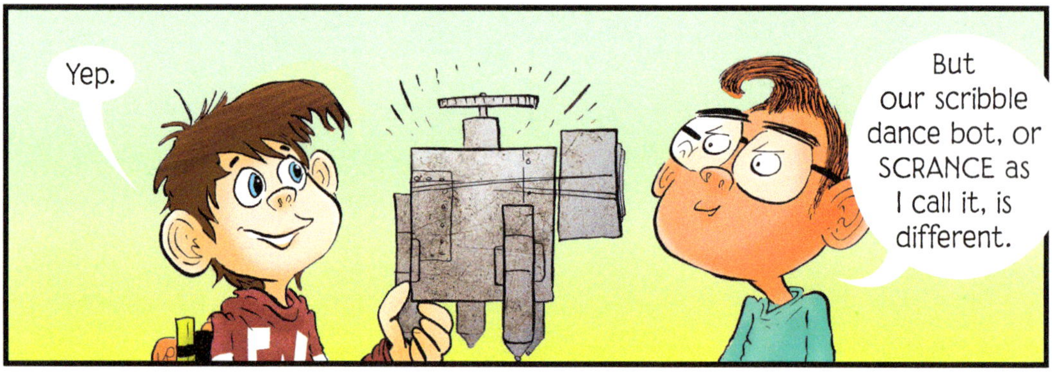
Yep.
But our scribble dance bot, or SCRANCE as I call it, is different.

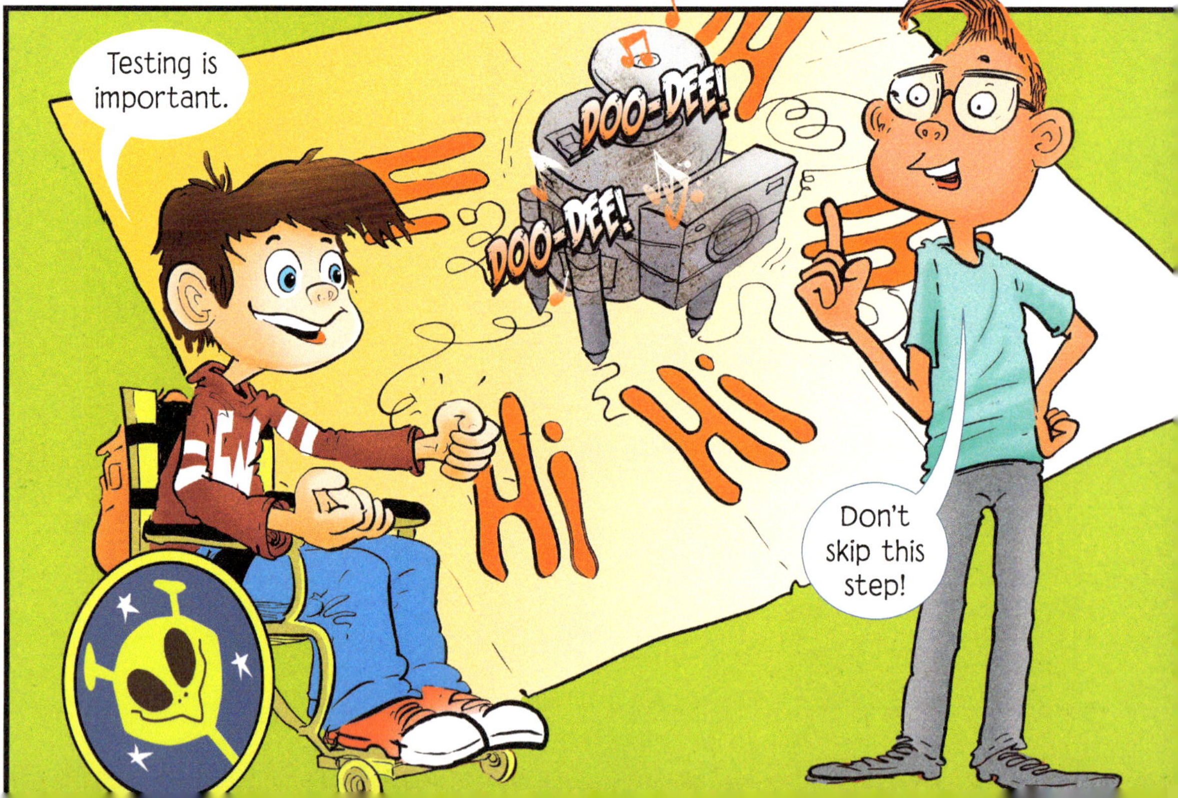
Testing is important.
DOO-DEE!
DOO-DEE!
Hi
Hi
Don't skip this step!

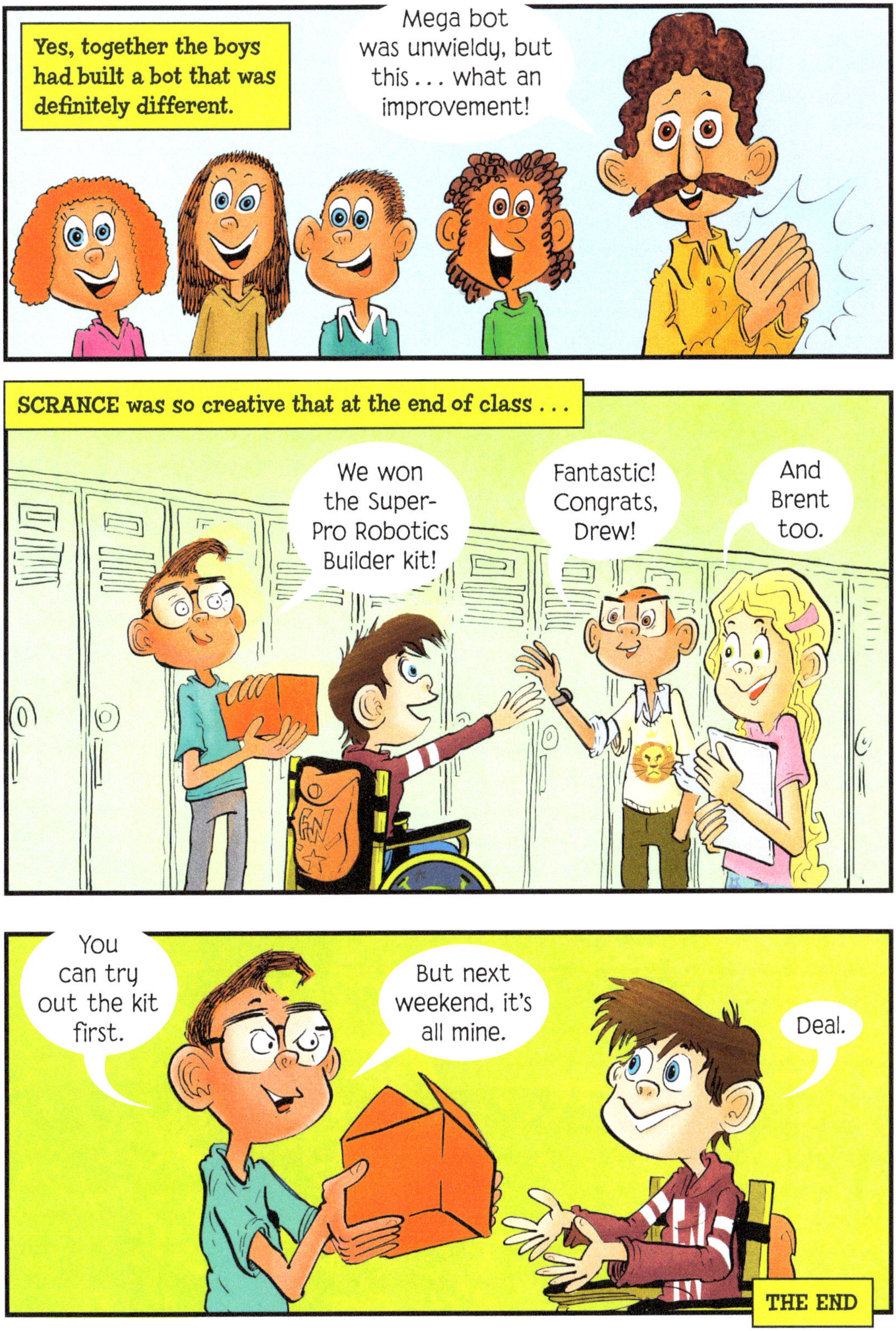
Yes, together the boys had built a bot that was definitely different.
Mega bot was unwieldy, but this . . . what an improvement!
SCRANCE was so creative that at the end of class . . .
We won the Super-Pro Robotics Builder kit!
Fantastic! Congrats, Drew!
And Brent too.
You can try out the kit first.
But next weekend, it's all mine.
Deal.
THE END

About the Author

Like Freewheeler, MOLLY FELDER has cerebral palsy and uses a wheelchair. She received her BA and MA in writing from NYU Gallatin. Her debut picture book, *Henry the Boy* (Penny Candy Books), is based on the years she spent walking with crutches. The Fantastic Freewheeler books are her first graphic novels. She loves having her service dog, Patterson, by her side. If she could choose a superpower, it would be to hear what he is thinking. They live in Alabama.

About the Illustrator

RORY WALKER is an artist and illustrator living in west Britain. He creates artwork for clients around the world and loves every second of it. Equally happy with a dip pen and a bottle of ink, a palette full of oil paints and a blank canvas, or a collection of archaic printmaking tools and a press, for him the act of creation is a constant pleasure. Other loves include making music and learning new culinary skills in the kitchen. He's generally happiest when running around big mountains, scurrying through forests, or swimming in lakes. Or whilst having a good chat.

Glossary

absorb (ab-ZORB)—to take in or suck up

afford (uh-FORD)—to have enough money to buy something

cerebral palsy (suh-REE-bruhl PAWL-zee)—a disability caused by damage to the brain before, during, or shortly after birth that affects a person's muscles and coordination

creative (kree-EY-tiv)—new and original and something that hasn't been seen before

elective (ih-LEK-tiv)—a course that students can choose to take but are not required to

expert (EK-spurt)—a person with great knowledge in something

fuse (FYOOZ)—to join together, especially through heat, pressure, or a chemical process

impress (im-PRESS)—to cause someone to think well of you

kinetic (kih-NET-ik)—of or relating to movement

redesign (ree-dih-ZAHYN)—something that has been changed and built differently, usually in order to make it better

rogue (ROHG)—when something goes rogue, it acts by itself in a wild, uncontrollable, and often dangerous way

shift (SHIFT)—a set amount of time to work

unwieldy (uhn-WEEL-dee)—difficult to handle, manage, or use

READ THEM ALL!

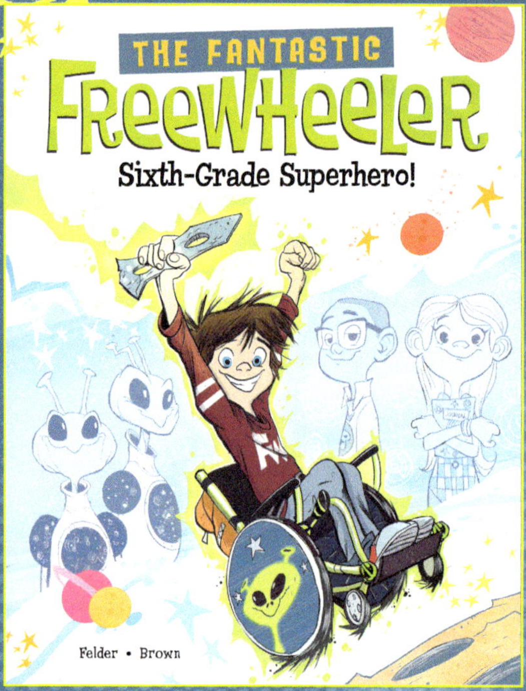
THE FANTASTIC
FREEWHEELER
Sixth-Grade Superhero!
Felder • Brown

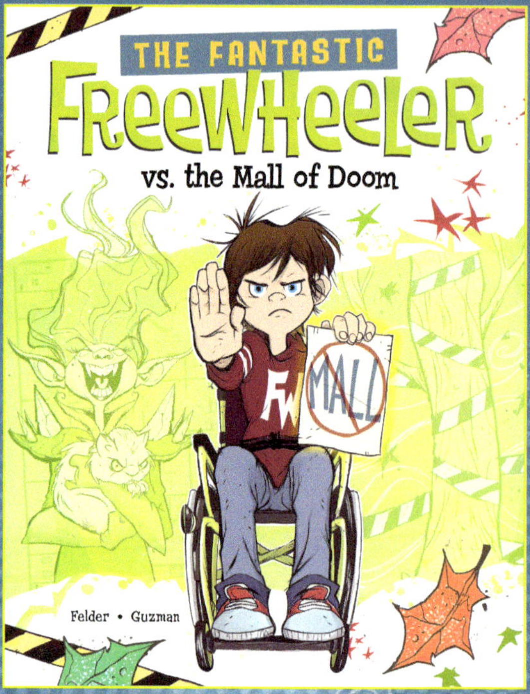
THE FANTASTIC
FREEWHEELER
vs. the Mall of Doom
MALL
Felder • Guzman

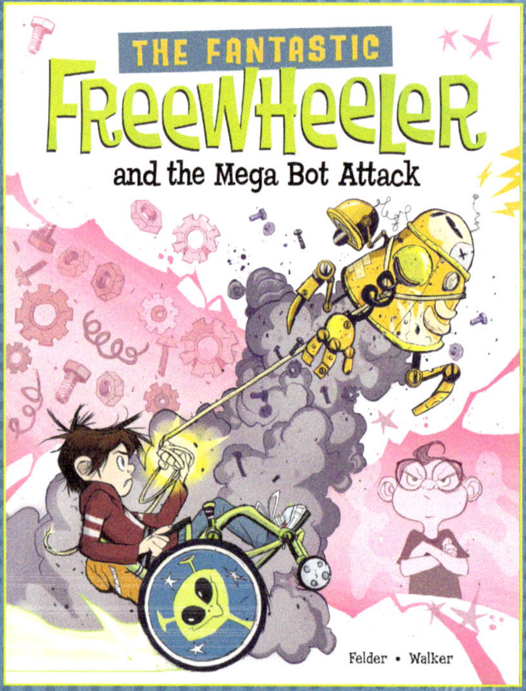
THE FANTASTIC
FREEWHEELER
and the Mega Bot Attack
Felder • Walker

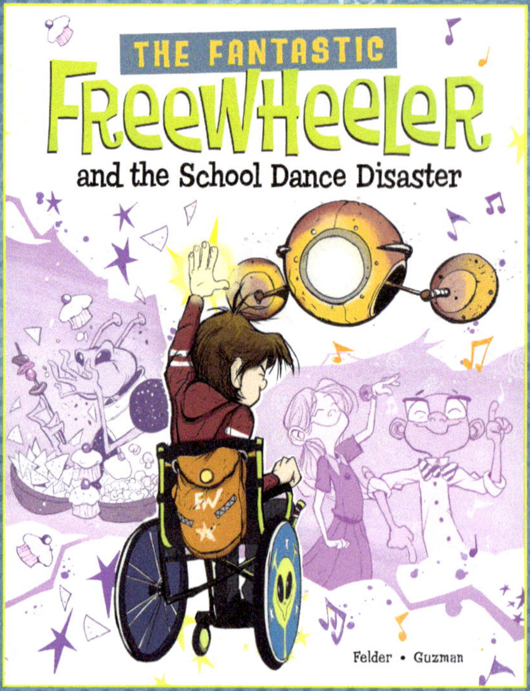
THE FANTASTIC
FREEWHEELER
and the School Dance Disaster
Felder • Guzman